"Tell them the truth, Marty," Zach said without looking away from the board. "Tell them we just launched an instructor and five Space Camp kids by mistake." He turned to look at Brennan. "Don't worry. No one will ever believe it."

"But the White House has to be told, too!" Brennan protested.

"Marty," Zach said, turning back to the board, "they'll be back in twelve hours."

"Zach," called one of the technicians, as he came up behind him. "We have to find an earlier reentry point."

"Why?" Zach asked, looking worried.

"The shuttle wasn't flight-ready," the technician said. "It's the oxygen. There isn't enough to last twelve hours."

SPACECAMP

ABC MOTION PICTURES Presents

A LEONARD GOLDBERG PRODUCTION   SPACECAMP

Starring KATE CAPSHAW   LEA THOMPSON   KELLY PRESTON   LARRY B. SCOTT   LEAF PHOENIX

Introducing TATE DONOVAN as "KEVIN" with TOM SKERRITT as "ZACH"

Production Designer RICHARD MACDONALD   Director of Photography WILLIAM A. FRAKER, A.S.C.

Music by JOHN WILLIAMS   Executive Producer LEONARD GOLDBERG

Screenplay by W. W. Wicket and CASEY T. MITCHELL

Story by PATRICK BAILEY and LARRY B. WILLIAMS

 Produced by PATRICK BAILEY and WALTER COBLENZ   Directed by HARRY WINER

[READ THE SCHOLASTIC BOOK]

point ™

SPACECAMP

A novelization by Joe Claro.

Based on the screenplay by W.W. Wicket
and Casey T. Mitchell and story by
Patrick Bailey and Larry B. Williams.

SCHOLASTIC INC.
New York Toronto London Auckland Sydney

This book is for Chris, Danielle, Noel, Nicole, and Tasha.

ISBN 0-590-40385-0

12 11 10 9 8 7 6 5 4 3 2   6 7 8 9/8 0 1/9

PROLOGUE
MAY 16, 1963

It's a beautiful spring evening, just on the verge of night. Andie Wickman, nine years old, is lying on her back in the grass, within hearing distance of her house. Inside the house, her parents and her two older brothers are watching TV.

Andie, however, is watching the stars. Millions — billions — *trillions* of stars, all of them shining and winking at her. And she's lying there watching for something.

Then, a streak of light flashes across the sky. Andie jumps to her feet with excitement. After a few seconds, she eases herself back down to the grass.

"Just a shooting star," she says, disappointed.

From a distance, she can hear a porch door creak. She knows who is at the door, and whose voice she's about to hear. She lies there, staring at the stars.

"Andie!" her mother calls. "Come on, Andie. We're all watching it on TV."

Andie gives a little snort, to show her private disdain for anyone who's watching it on TV.

"Andie? Come on, dear. You can't see it if you don't come in."

"I can, too," Andie says softly. She hears the porch door close. "Mothers!" she says to herself, shaking her head.

She still stares. As the sky grows darker, those trillions of stars shine more and more brightly. In the corner of her eye, she sees another streak of light. She tilts her head, then sighs with disappointment.

"Another shooting star," she mumbles.

But not this time. This time, she's wrong. The streak doesn't fade, the way shooting stars do. It keeps shining and moving across the stars.

Andie sits up, her eyes widening. This could be it. *This could actually be it!*

Now she's on her feet, her eyes glued to the white light that moves on a straight and steady course across her sky. Andie's sky. Andie's stars. And this beautiful white light is Andie's, too.

Then, the light blinks. It goes out. In a second, it comes back on again. And Andie's voice rings out across the field.

"He winked at me! Gordon Cooper winked at me!"

The porch door creaks again. Her mother makes her way toward Andie. But Andie is up in those stars with Gordon Cooper.

"He winked at me," she says.

"I know, dear," her mother replies. "Just like John Glenn winked at you last year."

They walk silently toward the house. Then Andie looks at the stars and says, quite matter-of-factly, "I'm going up."

"Maybe someday, dear," her mother says, leading her back to the house. "Right now, you aren't going anywhere but upstairs to take your bath."

"Am, too," Andie says. "I am, too, going up."

Never had she been so sure of anything in her whole life.

Chapter 1

"You're not going up, Andie. . . ."

Andie walked out of the NASA building five long paces ahead of her husband, Zach Bergstrom. It was now more than twenty years past that spring evening in 1963, and Andie had completed training to be a real astronaut. She strode toward the parking lot, each step an angry reflection of her mood. Zach left the building and hurried to catch up with her.

"So you didn't get this shuttle flight. You'll get your chance eventually. You know you will."

She stepped up her pace even faster. "Easy for you to say," she challenged. "You've been up. You got to walk on the moon your first time out." She reached into her purse and came up with her car keys, adding still more speed to her walk.

"Come on," Zach said, trying to get in front of her and catch her eye. "I had to wait seven long years before I was selected. And I didn't have a loving husband around to keep telling me it would all be okay."

Andie shot him a glance, and he grinned. "Well, Neil Armstrong *was* kind of supportive," he added.

"Zach, this means so much to me," she said. They had reached their car, a '59 Porsche, and she unlocked the driver's door and climbed inside. She reached over and unlocked the opposite door, and Zach got in.

"Look, Andie, neither of us can change the selection process. They turned you down this time. That leaves you with me. And with SpaceCamp."

Andie turned the ignition key. "Space-Camp," she sighed. "I get to play 'make-believe astronaut' with a bunch of kids."

She threw the car into reverse and backed out of the parking spot with a squeal of tires.

They rode in silence for a few minutes along the access road that led to the highway. Zach waited until he thought he sensed a change in Andie's mood.

Then he said, "Don't knock the kids, honey. They're the future."

"No," she said, shaking her head slowly. "*I'm* the future! After I've been up, then they can be the future!"

"You're going to love them," Zach said.

"Sure I am. All those average, clean-cut, All-American . . . kids!"

Chapter 2

As Andie drove across an intersection, she and Zach heard the squeal of tires behind them. She drove on with only a brief glance in her rearview mirror. The squeal was coming from a Jeep tearing across the intersection.

It was, in fact, a customized Jeep convertible, and it was on its way to the same place Andie and Zach were heading. The blare of an Eric Clapton tune announced the Jeep's presence to anyone within hearing.

The convertible was being piloted by Kevin Donaldson, a high school senior with a deep tan, a cool pair of shades, and a firm conviction that the world dearly loved him. Kevin sang along with Eric Clapton as he followed the signs leading him to what would be his summer home.

He didn't smile when he finally came to a sign at the entrance to a parking lot. UNITED STATES SPACECAMP — EST. 1982, it said.

"Home, sweet home," he muttered and hung a left into the lot.

Without ever having formulated the thought, Kevin had expected to be the first arrival at SpaceCamp. So he was a little disappointed to find the parking lot filled with cars and with families saying good-bye to the people he'd be spending the next three weeks with. He had hoped to make an entrance. Instead, he had to hunt for a parking spot.

He didn't hunt for long. He simply ignored the sign that said NASA OFFICIALS ONLY, and pulled into an empty space. He turned off the ignition, but left the music playing so he could hear "Same Old Blues" to the end. He turned and threw his legs onto the front seat, rested his head on the driver's door, and grinned at the sky while the sound of Clapton filled the parking lot.

Andie pulled the Porsche up behind the Jeep. "Well," she said to Zach, "what have we here? Looks like the future to me."

She got out of the car, leaving the motor running. She grinned at Zach, then turned and walked toward the camp. Zach slid over to the driver's seat and turned off the engine.

Kevin's fingers snapped along with the nearly deafening sound of the tape. Zach got out and stood over him, staring down into the reflecting sunglasses. Were the eyes behind the glasses open or closed?

"Hey!" Zach yelled.

Kevin removed the shades and grinned. "Hey," he said, returning what he thought was a greeting.

"Would you mind turning that down?" Zach yelled.

"No sweat," Kevin said, smiling. He reached over and turned the volume dial a tiny fraction of an inch. Zach reached into the car and turned it all the way down.

The silence seemed to startle Kevin. He sat up and looked at this strange creature who thought nothing of cutting off the sound of Clapton.

"You want SpaceCamp?" the creature asked.

"No," Kevin said thoughtfully. "My father wants SpaceCamp. *I* wanted this car." Then, with a smile, he added, "I figure it was a pretty good deal."

"Let's hope so," Zach said. "Shouldn't you be getting signed in, like everybody else?"

"Soon as this song is finished," Kevin said, reaching for the volume dial. "Okay if I turn up the sound? Or is there some federal regulation against playing The Man the way he's supposed to be played?"

Zach smiled. Then he moved his head toward Kevin, leaned on the door of the Jeep, and said, "No *federal* regulation against it. But if I had those dinky speakers of yours, I'd be embarrassed to play anything very loud. Unless you don't care that you're chopping the high end off one of the finest guitar sounds in the world."

Kevin's eyebrows moved up. He swallowed hard and stared up at the face of the older man.

Zach let some seconds go by. Then he added quietly, "And, by the way, get this toy fire engine out of my parking space."

For the first time, Kevin noticed the Porsche behind his car. He smiled sheepishly, turned on the ignition, and slowly began to back out around the Porsche.

The sudden roar of a low-flying plane had him and Zach craning their necks. Painted on the side of the plane was the message: FAIRLY CROP DUSTING. It was coming in for a landing.

Chapter 3

The plane passed low over the parking lot, over the administration building, and over the field where it would have to land. Then it circled around, dipped, and headed back to the field. Kevin watched from his car as the plane eased down, touched the ground, raced for a few seconds, then slowly came to a stop.

The pilot climbed out of the plane, removed her helmet and leather flight jacket, and handed them to the man in the passenger seat. In the distance, she noticed a boy hop out of a Jeep in the parking lot and begin trotting toward the plane.

"Thanks, Dad," Kathryn Fairly said. "And have a safe flight home."

Mr. Fairly climbed out of the plane and gave his daughter a hug. "You have some fun this summer, darling," he said.

"That isn't what I'm here for," she said, kissing him on the cheek.

They hugged again. Then she turned, picked up her bag, waved to him, and strode toward the administration building. Halfway there, she stopped to give her father another wave. When she turned toward the building again, she found herself face-to-face with a deep tan, and a pair of reflecting sunglasses.

"Hi. I'm Shuttle Commander Kevin Donaldson. Welcome to SpaceCamp."

Kathryn took two steps back, so she could walk around this obstruction. "Shuttle Commander," she said flatly.

"At your service," Kevin said, gesturing with a wide bow.

"Great," Kathryn said, adjusting her bag on her shoulder. She nodded toward the plane. "Check the oil and tires, and fill it with one hundred low-lead."

As she stepped around him, Kevin saw that her T-shirt carried the message: IF WE CAN SEND A MAN TO THE MOON. . . .

"Hey," he said, trying to preserve some of his dignity, "I know it's tough meeting a legend face-to-face — "

"And don't forget the windshield," she called over her shoulder.

Now he could see the second part of the message, printed on the back of her shirt: WHY CAN'T WE SEND THEM ALL?

"Hey!" Kevin called out. Then, more to himself, "I accept that. I'm good at rejection. I really am."

Back in the parking lot, Tish Ambrose was doing what she could to get her parents to leave. Tish stood out in the parking lot, as she stood out almost everywhere she went.

Her frizzy, bleached-blonde curls, the three sets of unmatched earrings in each ear, a dozen plastic bracelets of various pastel colors on each wrist, the torn T-shirt, and the tight skirt — all combined to make Tish a visual phenomenon similar to a shooting star.

She was gathering up her bags, when her father said, "Tish, are you sure you wouldn't rather come to the cabin with us?"

Tish looked up at him, apparently confused by what he had in mind. "You mean — " she struggled for the right words. "You mean, go on a vacation with my *parents*?"

"Well — yes," her father said, befuddled. "Your mother — me — yes, your parents."

"What your father is trying to say," Mrs. Ambrose interjected, "is that we love you, hon."

"Right," Tish said. "I love you, too. But let's not get gruesome about it, you know what I mean?"

She gave each of them a peck on the cheek, picked up her luggage, and hurried toward the building.

* * *

Rudy Tyler was having a similar problem getting away from his family. He had to contend not only with his parents, but with a younger brother and sister who had been talking all week about how they were going to miss him.

Mr. Tyler made one last stab. "Rudy, you're sure this is how you want to spend the summer?"

"Am I sure?" Rudy began. "Am I *sure*? Is Magic Johnson an athlete? Does a bear live in the woods? Does the moon shine at night? How can you ask me a question like that, Dad? Do I want this chance to learn about the space program? Do I want to someday become the fourth, maybe the fifth black man in space?"

As his voice rose, his parents became just a bit embarrassed at the possibility that everyone in the parking lot was listening to their son.

"Do I want the opportunity to represent my country in what may be the most exciting challenge of this century — and the next? Do I want — "

Mr. Tyler waited patiently for his son to finish. "A simple yes or no would have sufficed," he said softly.

Father and son shared a hug. "Have a nice summer," Mr. Tyler said.

As Rudy made his way toward the building, a counselor walked around the parking lot with a bullhorn.

"Okay, let's go. Orientation is about to begin. Moms and dads, time to say good-bye. You'll be getting your sons and daughters back in three weeks. We'll try not to do too much damage."

Chapter 4

The campers moved into the building alone or in small groups. The counselors were waiting for them in the lobby, in front of an auditorium, standing behind long tables with stacks of badges, hats, and cloth bags. On one table, everything was blue, the next was red, then green, and then white.

Kevin remembered that his letter of acceptance had told him he'd be on the red team. He took a step in the direction of the red table, then stopped when he saw Kathryn picking up her blue gear.

He got on the blue line behind a boy who had just put a blue tag on the table. The boy was looking through his wallet for something. Kevin put his red tag on the table and slipped the boy's blue tag into his hand.

"Come on, kids," a counselor called out from behind the table. "Let's get a move on."

Kevin moved ahead on the line. The counselor behind the table pushed a pile toward him — a blue cap, a blue badge, and a blue camp bag. Kevin smiled at him, picked up the gear, and followed Kathryn into the small auditorium.

"Leave your luggage in the lobby," a counselor announced. "Please step it up, kids."

Kevin walked into the darkened auditorium, where he found himself nearly surrounded by photographic images from space. There were ten separate screens, and the image on each screen changed every few seconds. Some were moving pictures, some were still photos, and the rapid changes made it impossible to concentrate on any single one for very long.

Kevin stood near the entrance, giving his eyes a chance to adapt to the darkness. The "oohs" and "aahs" came from all around him. After a few seconds, he could see a bit better, and he moved into the room, looking for Kathryn. When he found her, he squeezed into her row and sat next to her.

"Hi, there," he said, his face as close to hers as he dared to put it.

Her eyes darted from one screen image to another. "Isn't this terrific?" she asked.

"It sure is," he said softly, inching his head a little closer to hers.

"There's Sullivan!" Kathryn said, pointing. "And Parker! And Bergstrom on his fifth flight! Wow, this is great!"

Kevin made a face at her in the dark. He pulled away from her and slouched down into his seat.

"Some competition," he mumbled. "Pictures of old guys in space suits."

Then, one by one, the screens went dark. When the last one went out, the houselights came on, and the ten screens rose toward the ceiling to reveal a small stage with a podium on it. As Zach Bergstrom walked toward the podium, the room filled with applause. Andie stood in the back of the theater, smiling at the ovation her husband was getting.

With the room lighted, Kathryn turned to look at the person sitting next to her. "You?" she said weakly, not able even to pretend that the surprise was pleasant.

"Yep," Kevin said brightly, sitting up straight and looking her in the eye. "It must be fate throwing us together."

"Right," Kathryn said, turning her attention back to the podium. "My horoscope said this would be a bad day."

Kevin would have responded, but Zach was ready to speak.

"Thank you," he said. "My name is Zach Bergstrom, and I'm the director of Space-Camp."

There was another round of mild applause. Zach gave the audience a smile of gratitude and continued.

"As you know, anyone can come to SpaceCamp. Some of you, I'm sure, aced physics. Some of you cut physics. And some of you think physics is the build on the kid sitting next to you."

Some people in the audience laughed. Many more of them groaned, as Zach had expected them to.

"But whatever your background," he went on, "the future is in space. And *you* are the future."

He looked at Andie, standing near the entrance. She nodded slightly.

"At SpaceCamp, we want to give you people of varying backgrounds a common goal. You're here to learn not just the technical stuff, but how to work as a team."

Down in the third row, Kevin whispered a comment to Kathryn. She stared in awe at Zach and never heard a word Kevin said.

"We're going to train you," Zach said, "just like NASA trains astronauts. Check that out, please. I don't say 'real' astronauts because as far as we at SpaceCamp are concerned, you *are* real astronauts."

There was a murmur from some people in the audience. Kevin looked around him, feeling like a stranger amid all this emotion. Kathryn never took her eyes off Zach.

"You've all been assigned to crews, which are designated by color. For the next three weeks, you and your fellow crew members will eat together, think together, and breathe together." Zach paused to let his gaze cover everyone in the audience. Then he asked, "Are there any questions?"

Kevin shot his hand into the air. Zach nodded to him, and he stood up. Kathryn, and everyone else, looked at him.

"I have a question, sir," he said, putting his hand on Kathryn's shoulder. "My teammate here would like to know if she and I will get any time to be alone."

Zach smiled, the audience laughed loudly, and Kathryn's face turned a shade of red that Kevin had never seen before. He instantly regretted what he'd done. But not enough to let her know it.

He gave her a big, silly-looking grin and pulled his cap from his back pocket. "We're on the same team," he said.

She pushed past him and hurried up the aisle.

Chapter 5

Twenty minutes later, several groups — all color-coordinated — had formed in the open area outside the administration building. To a casual observer, two things separated the blue group from all the others. One, their team leader was a woman. Two, the team had a member who was dancing in place to a beat that only she could hear — through her stereo headphones.

"Please turn that thing off," Andie said, pointing to the state-of-the-art laser disc player Tish wore around her neck. Looking a bit surprised at the request, Tish flipped a button and cut off the music.

Andie tapped her clipboard.

"I'm Andie Bergstrom, your team leader."

"Andie Bergstrom!" Kathryn blurted. "You're an astronaut! First female shuttle pilot!"

Andie looked at her for a few seconds. Then

she said, "I hope to be. How did you know that?"

"I read about you," Kathryn said, staring at her celebrity team leader. "In the Young Astronauts Program. You were backup pilot on the first Discovery flight, but Coats got it instead."

Some of the color seemed to drain from Andie's face. "Yes," she said coolly. "I remember."

"I'm sorry," Kathryn said hurriedly. "I didn't mean — "

"That's all right," Andie said with a little smile. "The disappointment is my problem, not yours."

Kathryn's face was bright red for the second time in less than an hour. Andie turned to talk to Rudy, who was nervously chewing gum as though it were an Olympic sport.

"Hello," Andie said. "What's your name?"

"Yes, ma'am," Rudy said, straightening up and slapping his hands at his sides. "Rudy Tyler, ma'am."

"Spit it out, Rudy," she said.

In response, Rudy threw his head back, pulled in his stomach, and announced, "RUDY! TYLER! MA'AM!"

Andie gaped at him, then realized he had misunderstood her last remark. "I meant the gum, Rudy," she said.

Rudy nodded.

"Okay, Rudy," Andie said. "You seem to have a lot of energy. I'm going to make you mission specialist in charge of equipment function and operation."

Rudy swallowed hard, accidentally swallowing his gum. "Ma'am," he said finally, "uh, I'm not real good under pressure."

"You'll do fine," Andie said, smiling. "Oh, and Rudy, this is SpaceCamp, not the Marine Corps. The name is Andie."

She turned from Rudy's weak smile to one that could have lit up the administration building at midnight. This smile was surrounded by earrings, bracelets, and a silenced laser disc player.

"Hi, Andie. I'm Tish? Tish Ambrose?"

Andie recognized the speech pattern right away. Tish, she decided, would use more question marks in an hour than a lawyer during a year's worth of cross-examination.

"Hello, Tish," Andie said with a smile. "Tell me, what brings you to SpaceCamp?"

"I sat in last year on this class in radio astronomy? At the Jet Propulsion Lab? It was unreal, you know? Listening to radio waves from space? I mean, like waiting for signs of intelligence?"

Andie stared at this highly unlikely SpaceCamper. Then she said, "Like, I know the feeling, Tish." Her eyes crinkled into a little smile as she added, "You're mission specialist number two. In charge of communications."

She made a note on her clipboard and moved down the line. She had to look down toward the ground to see the next blue hat. There he was, four feet ten inches high, looking out at the horizon with his feet spread and his hands clasped behind his back. Andie rolled her eyes toward the sky, sighed, and looked the short member in the eye.

"Max Graham," she said, "what are you doing here?"

Eyes fixed firmly on the horizon, Max responded, "Checking in for my next mission against the Empire, Your Highness."

The others giggled at this.

"It's a pint-sized Luke Skywalker," Kevin said.

"Max," Andie said patiently, "your only mission is to get yourself back to Junior Camp where you belong."

"Come on, Andie!" Max said, stepping out of character and revealing his true identity. "I've been a junior two summers now. You know I can handle more than Junior Camp. Those are just kids over there!"

"How old are you now, Max?" Andie asked.

"What is this?" Max demanded. "Age discrimination? I'm twelve. What of it?"

"How *tall* are you now, Max?" Andie went on.

"One-point-four-seven meters. And growing."

"You're just not ready," Andie said sympathetically.

"I am, too, ready!" Max said fiercely.

For a few seconds, everything in Andie's mind was wiped out by the memory of a nine-year-old girl staring up at the stars. She understood what this meant to Max.

"Okay, Max," she said. "We'll give it a try. You'll be the payload specialist. But one mistake, and we ship you right back where you came from. Got it?"

Max smiled. "I copy you, Rogue Leader," he said. "Over and out."

Andie glanced at her clipboard, then ran her eyes over the group. With a look of slight confusion, she asked, "Hideo Takamini?"

Kevin looked around the group. Then he suddenly remembered switching colored tags with the kid on the blue line. That must have been Hideo Takamini. Kevin stepped forward and smiled at Andie.

"Kevin Donaldson," he said brightly.

"I don't have a Donaldson — "

"You have now," he grinned.

Andie looked at him and added his name to her list. Then she turned to Kathryn.

"I'm Kathryn Fairly. It's an honor to meet you."

Andie nodded and said, "Two positions are

left. Pilot and shuttle commander. Kevin, tell me why you'd like to be commander."

"I wouldn't," Kevin answered. "I was thinking more along the lines of mission sovereign. Intergalactic emperor, maybe. Something along those lines."

Andie turned back to Kathryn.

Kathryn looked her in the eye and spoke quietly. "I enjoy responsibility. I know a lot about the space program. I'm going to the Air Force Academy. And I can do the job."

Andie returned her gaze, recognizing herself at the same age. "Do you think it's the most important job?" she asked.

After a short pause, Kathryn said, "Yes, I do."

"It's okay," Kevin said lightly. "Let her have it. I really don't care."

"Is that right?" Andie said. "Well, now that you're shuttle commander, you're going to have to start to care, aren't you? Kathryn, I'm appointing you pilot."

The other groups were filing off to their sleeping quarters now, and the sun was beginning to sink. Andie stuck her pen into a shirt pocket and looked over her whole group.

"All right, hit the dorms," she said. "I'll meet you in Building A in thirty minutes."

They watched Andie stride off, then began to collect their bags. They moved more or less in a group toward the dormitories, Kevin trying to catch Kathryn's eye, Rudy tripping every now and then over his numerous bags, Max moving with a military bearing, and Tish bopping along to the music once again coming from her player.

When they reached the dorm area, Rudy stopped at a soft drink machine and fished in his pockets. "Anybody got a quarter?" he called out.

"That won't be necessary," Max announced.

The whole group stopped to watch as Max stepped up to the machine and hit the selection buttons in quick succession: one, two, three, one, three, four, five. Then he gave a quick bang with his fist to the side of the machine and stepped back. After a five-second pause, a stream of cans began rolling out of the machine.

All eyes moved from the machine to the shortest member of the group. Max picked up his bags and headed for the dorm entrance.

"Don't everybody thank me at once," he called over his shoulder.

Chapter 6

It was called a shuttle simulator, but the name didn't matter to most of them. As far as they were concerned, they were inside a space shuttle. They'd all seen the shuttle on TV. Most of them had spent hours reading about it and studying pictures of it. They knew a shuttle when they walked into one.

Andie waited until the sounds of appreciation had died down. Then she began her opening lecture.

"This is the shuttle simulator," she said. "You're going to learn to fly this machine at speeds beyond Mach One, which, incidentally, is the speed of sound."

Eyes wide, Tish said, "My Rabbit only does sixty-five."

"You like to drive, Tish?" Andie asked. "Then you won't have any problems with this." She raised her voice to address everyone. "I know it looks complicated right now. But once you get the basics, it's no more complicated than driving a car. The computer does most of the work."

While they continued to stare at the awesome machine, Andie stepped up to it. "All right," she said, "let's get started with your first lesson. It's called — "

She didn't finish because the simulator suddenly tilted ninety degrees to the right on its hydraulic base. Then, just as suddenly, it flipped back level again.

Andie was the first to regain her balance, and she knew just where to look for the cause of the trouble. She saw the switch, and she saw Rudy standing right next to it, looking as though he had just accidentally wiped out a couple of planets.

"Your first lesson," she went on, as though she hadn't been interrupted at all, "is 'Why I Won't Touch Anything Until I Know How To Use It.' " To be sure her point had been made, she lightly tapped Rudy on the hand.

An hour later, Andie was leading the crew through the Space Museum. Dozens of DO NOT TOUCH signs throughout the museum reminded them of their first lesson. Andie was pointing out some exhibits from the Mercury, Gemini, and Apollo ships.

For Kevin, it was all a bit slow and boring. He wandered away from the group, yawning and looking aimlessly around the room. Ignoring one of the DO NOT TOUCH signs, he leaned his back against the Mercury capsule, as though it were a storefront in his local shopping center.

SLAP!

Something slammed across his chest, and a sound he'd never heard in a shopping center rang in his ears.

The sound brought the crew members running in his direction. They saw a pale-faced Kevin pinned to the side of the capsule by a spidery metal arm.

"What's going on?" Kevin asked feebly.

Max reached him first. When he saw what the situation was, he stopped running and started laughing.

Everyone else stopped running then and tried to figure out what Max found so funny. A small round metal object rose slowly behind Kevin's head, but only Max thought that this added more humor to the moment.

The small round object had two blinking red lights, which looked like the eyes in an alien creature from a sci-fi movie. As it rose above Kevin's head, it became clear that it was connected to the same large, round, white body as the arm that was pinning him to the capsule.

The crew watched as the blinking red lights scanned the room, then stopped on Max. "Hello, Jinx," Max said.

Once again, the crew stared openmouthed at

Max. He let some seconds pass, as he enjoyed the attention. Then he turned to them and explained.

"Prototype Maintenance Android," he said. "NASA built this robot for the space station. He probably knows more about the whole space program than any single astronaut."

"When is he going up?" Rudy asked.

"He isn't," Max said, looking over at Jinx. "They found out that his shielding wouldn't withstand the heat. He'd lose his chips in about two hours."

Andie, who had now joined the group, added, "He helps out around here and out at the Cape. Jinx is the world's only twenty-seven-million-dollar handyman."

"This is all very interesting," Kevin said, "but just how do I — "

"Jinx!" a voice called. It sounded as though it was coming from underground.

The spidery arm slid back into the round metal body, and Kevin quickly stepped away from the capsule. Beneath the round body Jinx had three legs similar to his two arms. At the bottom of each leg was a roller.

Max shook his head in sympathy as Jinx rolled away. All that intelligence, all that power, being used to fetch and carry, as though Jinx were nothing more than a bright dog.

Jinx rolled over to a tool kit, extended an arm, and withdrew a ratchet wrench. Then he rolled over to a capsule in an exhibit that was only half constructed.

"Jinx! Where's that ratchet?" the voice called out in annoyance.

The hand of an unseen mechanic reached out from under the capsule, and Jinx smartly slapped the wrench into the open palm.

"In your hand," Jinx said, a remark that brought a laugh from the blue team.

"He's very literal," Andie explained. "He may not always understand what you mean. But he'll always react to exactly what you've said."

Max smiled as Jinx rolled off to another part of the museum. Is it possible, he wondered, to think of a droid as a friend?

Chapter 7

On the first night, the dorms had been filled with dozens of individuals, each trying to adjust to the new surroundings. Now, on their second night together, most of the campers were more comfortable with one another, feeling a bit more at home.

In the girls' dorm, Tish was stretched out on an upper bunk, eyes closed, head bobbing in time to the music that came softly from her laser disc player. In the lower bunk, Kathryn painfully pored over a series of diagrams that were spread all over her bed.

Three other girls sat in the middle of the floor playing a trivia board game. One of them turned up a card and read, "What will appear when the sun activates your melanocytes?"

The two other players looked stumped. Without opening her eyes, Tish called out from her bunk, "Freckles."

"What?" one of the players asked.

"Freckles," Tish repeated, sitting up on an elbow. "Melanocytes are those things that carry pigmentation? And the pigmentation shows up on your skin — you know — as freckles?"

"She's right," said the girl with the card. All three players stared at Tish in amazement.

Tish rolled to the edge of the mattress and let her head hang over. "That Kevin is a real babe," she said to Kathryn.

"He's a jerk," Kathryn said without looking up from her diagrams.

"His shoulders take my breath away, you know what I mean?" Tish said.

Kathryn continued to stare at her papers. Tish waved a hand in front of her face.

"Earth to Kathryn," she said. "Come in, Kathryn. What are you doing, anyway?"

Kathryn looked up at the dangling head for the first time. "I'm trying to figure out how to run this thing," Kathryn answered.

Tish swung herself around and landed feet first on the floor. Then she slid onto Kathryn's bunk and glanced at the diagrams.

"Multi-axis trainer?" she said. "Three concentric circles spinning in different directions simultaneously. The object is to stabilize from a central point, using hand controls."

Kathryn looked hard at her bunkmate. Then she squinted a little and looked even harder.

"How do you know all that?" she asked.

Tish shrugged. "I read it while I was waiting

for the shower after dinner. What's the problem?"

"It's one of the toughest things I've ever read," Kathryn said. "It's scary. Do you actually *remember* it?"

"Yep," Tish said, throwing her head back onto Kathryn's pillow. "I remember everything I read," she added casually.

"You have a photographic memory?"

"Yeah," Tish said, staring at her own mattress overhead. "And it's a real drag. I mean, my mind gets totally cluttered."

"What did you get on your SAT's?" asked Kathryn.

"Eight hundreds. You ever talk about anything besides school stuff?"

When Kathryn didn't answer, Tish looked over to find her staring in amazement. Tish stared back for a few seconds.

"You know, you're real pretty," Tish said finally, without even the hint of a question mark. "A little understated, though. Maybe I could do a makeup job on you. Your eyes, mostly. Guys go for eyes."

Kathryn studied the five-color decoration Tish wore on her own eyes. She tried to imagine wearing the same thing, with no success.

"Thanks," she said. "But makeup isn't going to do it. Guys go for what I haven't got."

"Not Kevin," Tish said smiling. "Whatever you've got, Kevin has gone flippo over it."

Chapter 8

"Space food," Rudy said, making a face as he looked at the two tubes in his hand. "It's going to be like eating toothpaste for dinner."

He and Kevin stepped out of the Space Canteen and headed along the lighted path toward the dorm.

"I asked for a cheeseburger and fries to go," Rudy said, looking disdainfully at the tubes. "Which one is the fries, I wonder?"

"Why didn't you get regular food, like everybody else?" asked Kevin.

"No way!" Rudy said excitedly. "I got to check out my competition!"

"How's that?" Kevin asked.

"I'm starting a fast-food franchise in space," Rudy said matter-of-factly. "The guys on a space station get a raving craving for a charbroiled burger and some golden fries, *I'm* gonna be there to satisfy it."

"Is that why you're here?" Kevin asked. He

saw Rudy take the deep breath that usually preceded one of his "presentations," and he jumped in to stop it.

"Without the rap," Kevin pleaded. "This time, just answer me straight. Okay?"

Rudy looked off into the distance for a few seconds. Then he answered.

"I like learning," he said quietly. "I hear what the dudes say in school. 'How come you're taking science, man? You don't have to take science.' They never ask me if I *like* science."

"Do you like science?" Kevin asked.

"Yeah," Rudy said. "Now ask me if I'm any good at it."

"Not so hot, huh?"

"The *worst*," Rudy said. "What it really is is the pressure. Me and pressure just don't get along."

"I know what you mean," Kevin said. "Now, the way I look at it, the best thing is to sleep late, drive fast, and don't take any of this stuff seriously."

"Now who's rappin'?" Rudy asked softly.

Kevin looked at him, nodded, and smiled. When they heard the shriek, they both tore in the direction of the dorm.

The scream had come from the boys' dorm. More specifically, it had come from the throat of Max, who was now trapped in a corner with Jinx behind him and three older campers from the green team closing in on him.

"Come on, kid," said Banning, the least threatening of the three. "We won't hurt it. We just want to check it out."

"Where did you get it, anyway?" Gardener asked. "Come on, let's have a look."

As they stepped closer, Max yelled, "No! Leave him alone!"

Then Crowe, the meanest of the three, stepped in front of the other two. "Outta my way, you little punk!" he shouted. "I want to see this thing!"

"What's going on?" Kevin yelled, stepping into the room with Rudy right behind him.

"The kid has this thing here — " Gardener began.

"Why don't you evaporate, laser-brain!" Max shouted in frustration.

Angered by the outburst, Crowe moved toward Max, who cringed in fear. Now Jinx was fully visible.

He had climbed up the wall to get away from the green team. The suction cups on his arms were holding him off the floor. Stripped of Max's protection, his head was scanning the room, and his red lights were flashing. High-pitched beeps came from the speaker in his head. This robot was either very angry, very frightened, or both.

"Holy Toledo!" Banning said.

"Toledo," Jinx's speaker said. "A small city

in Spain, a larger city in Ohio. Toledo, Ohio, has a population of four hundred thousand and covers an area of ninety-six square miles."

"Cancel, Jinx," Max said. "Get down from the wall."

Jinx stopped his recitation, then removed himself from the wall, one suction cup at a time. Kevin and Rudy had met the robot in the museum, so they took this pretty much in stride. The other three were astounded.

"What does it do?" Banning asked.

"Anything you ask him to," Max said.

"Moves slow for a robot," Crowe said.

"Hey, Jinx, shake a leg."

Living up to his literal reputation, Jinx began shaking his left leg and held it out for the boys' approval.

Gardener, a light bulb going on inside his head, cried, "Oh, man! You mean he does exactly what he's told!"

The three of them then went into a routine that had Jinx spinning all over the room.

"Hang a right, Jinx!"

"Hang a left!"

"What's up, Jinx?"

"Get down."

"Look up."

"Yeah, look up *confusion* in the dictionary!"

Jinx tried to follow each command, or what he understood each command to mean. The result was a robot veering in one direction, then the opposite, tilting his head up, then down, then spinning it in a circle, all the while emitting a series of high-pitched sounds.

"STOP IT!" Max screamed.

As Jinx began to wind down, Kevin yelled, "Hey, guys, that's enough!"

Jinx fell into a heap on the floor, his lights still shining, but no longer blinking. No sounds came from his head. Banning, Gardener, and Crowe moved wordlessly to the door and hurried away down the hall. Rudy stood in the doorway with Kevin.

Max moved to the metal heap in the middle of the floor and knelt beside it. He lifted Jinx by the body and cradled the head in his arms. Jinx's domelight pulsed once. Then all his lights went out. Max was very close to tears.

Kevin stepped up behind him and put his hand on Max's shoulder. "Sorry, kid," he said. Then he and Rudy walked away.

Max looked down at the "face" of the robot. "I'll show them," he whispered. Then, out loud, staring into Jinx's lifeless lights, *"We'll* show them!"

Chapter 9

Hours later, a lone light burned inside the Space Museum. The place was deadly silent, except for the occasional echo of a tool dropping to the floor.

The light was coming from the Viking exhibit, and it had been turned on by Max, who was working feverishly to get his metal friend back into shape. He knelt between Jinx and a toolbox, tightening screws, reconnecting wires, and testing circuits.

Spread out on the floor beside Max was a diagram of the inner workings of the Prototype Maintenance Android. Not many people would have been able to make any sense out of the diagram, but Max had two things going for him: He was an electronics marvel, and he was determined to get Jinx back into working order.

"Sensor generator okay," Max said after checking one section of Jinx's innards against the diagram.

"Image analysis is clean," he announced to himself, after another check.

Finally, he finished what he hoped would be the final step necessary for reviving Jinx. He tightened the last screw, took a deep breath, and stepped back. He looked down at the figure of Jinx, half lying, half sitting against the Viking exhibit.

Then he said softly, "Yo, Jinx?"

The silence lasted a few seconds, but to Max it felt like years. Then a whirring sound came from Jinx's speakers, followed by a beep, a whirr, and two more beeps.

The light on Jinx's dome began to glow, and he moved his body so that he was sitting up straight. His head spun in a full circle and scanned the room.

"Yo, Max," Jinx said.

Max clapped his hands together once and grinned. Then he bent down and began putting the tools back into the toolbox.

"I can't believe those green team idiots did that to you," he said, closing the box and locking it. "They ought to be zapped."

Jinx's domelight flashed. He raised himself onto his legs, turned toward the exit, and began rolling away.

"Jinx, where are you going?"

"To zap them," Jinx said, continuing toward the door.

"No, no, Jinx! Cancel!" Max said, running

over to him. Jinx stopped in his tracks.

"There you go again," Max said. "Why do you take everything so literally?"

After a short pause, Jinx said, "How else to take it?"

"Never mind," Max said, reminded again that he was dealing with a computer, not a human being. "It's okay, Jinx. You're really special."

"You are special, too, Max," Jinx responded.

Max smiled. He held out his hand and said, "Friends forever?"

Jinx extended one of his arms and grasped Max's hand. "Friends forever," he said.

They left the museum together, one walking, the other rolling. Both seemed to be moving with a little extra bounce.

Chapter 10

During the second week of SpaceCamp, the blue team began training on the same special machines that the astronauts had used to prepare for missions in space. Their schedule looked something like this:

SECOND WEEK, MONDAY: *Campers will work with "moonwalkers" to experience one sixth of their normal Earth weight.*

Andie stood watching as the crew, all in blue coveralls, experienced varying amounts of difficulty getting into the unfamiliar equipment. It was a task no one found easy the first time around.

"Do you sit in this thing or lie in it?" Rudy asked, grunting as he strapped himself into the chairlike machine that was suspended from above by a curved arm.

With their seat belts secured, both Kevin

and Rudy did what everyone does on first using moonwalkers. They jumped.

Ten or twelve feet in the air, they went floating past each other, grinning and yelping with delight. The feeling was just like walking on the moon. Kevin held his hand up for a high-five slap. Rudy did the same. In slow motion, they swung toward each other — and missed. They floated away in opposite directions.

SECOND WEEK, TUESDAY: *Campers will experience zero gravity by experimenting with the zero-g machine.*

"This looks like a ride I tried at an amusement park once," Tish said, as Andie strapped her into the contraption.

The zero-g machine looked something like the seat on a Ferris wheel, attached to a long pole. A bar clamped shut in front of the seat to give Tish something to hold on to.

"Remember to move carefully," Andie reminded her. "A movement in any direction just keeps going in that direction. The slightest push will send you sailing."

As the others watched, Tish gave what she thought was a gentle push. Not nearly gentle enough, it turned out. She shot upward almost sixty feet before she came to a stop.

Andie rushed over and helped bring her down.

"I think I saw my whole life flash before me,"

Tish said, turning greener by the second.

Andie looked at her and sighed.

SECOND WEEK, WEDNESDAY: *Campers will practice being Mission Control.*

Each crew member sat in front of a personal computer, typing at a keyboard and watching the screen for results. The Mission Operations Control Room was the nerve center that co-ordinated every part of the shuttle's flight. The room itself was dominated by a twenty-foot-high screen that showed a map of the world, on which was superimposed the flight path of a shuttle's orbit. It also displayed data that could be entered into the computers for processing.

Andie walked back and forth, checking the screens of her crew members. She stopped to watch Kathryn entering data with the speed of a trained professional. A small smile began to form on her lips, a smile that she immediately disposed of when Kathryn turned to look up at her.

She nodded at Kathryn and moved on to look at Tish's screen. Tish was pounding away at the keys, but her screen was blank.

"Stop typing for a minute," Andie said, putting her hand on Tish's shoulder.

Tish looked at Andie, who pointed to the electric cord that extended from the back of the computer. Tish followed Andie's hand, which traced the path of the wire over to the point where it was wrapped around Rudy's leg.

"Plug it in," Andie said, and moved on again.

The screen on Max's computer was filled with a complex design unlike anything Andie had ever seen before. "What is that?" she asked.

"High speed crisis vehicle maneuvering," Max answered, without looking up from his keyboard.

Impressed, Andie asked, "Where did you learn about that?"

"My final mission against the Death Star," Max said. "We blew it out of the galaxy."

Andie sighed and moved on.

At the next computer, Kevin's fingers were on the keyboard, but he was asleep. He opened his eyes when Andie cleared her throat.

"Where's your program?" she asked.

"*Days of Our Lives*," he said, half awake, "doesn't come on for another ten minutes."

SECOND WEEK, THURSDAY: *Campers will simulate the experience of bringing a tumbling spacecraft under control, by means of the multi-axis trainer.*

"As you can see," Andie explained, "the chair you'll be sitting in is connected to all three of these circles surrounding it. Once it starts to move, the chair might spin in any of those three directions. And it will shift from one axis to another in an unpredictable pattern."

"Oh, great," said Kevin, who was scheduled to be first up. "My stomach is already rebelling."

As Kevin strapped himself into the chair, Andie spoke to him and the others. "If the capsule starts spinning when it reenters Earth's atmosphere, it will behave something like what you're about to experience. The idea is to stabilize the movement by using the control stick on the right of the chair."

She checked to make sure that Kevin was securely strapped in. "Ready?" she asked.

"No," Kevin said grimly. "But you're going to start it whether I am or not."

Andie stepped to the side and threw the switch. Kevin began spinning in one direction, and within ten seconds he switched directions four times. The others laughed at his groaning. But no one laughed very hard, since they all knew they'd be in that same chair soon enough.

Andie threw the switch to stop the spinning. "The astronaut has only seconds to stabilize the craft, once it reenters the atmosphere. Kevin, you obviously would not have made it."

Kevin staggered away from the chair, nodding his acceptance of Andie's evaluation. He leaned his back against a wall, then slid down until he was sitting on the floor.

He watched Kathryn strapping herself into the chair. Then Andie threw the switch, and

Kathryn went into the same crazy spin that Kevin had just left.

"Grab your stick!" Andie yelled. "Use your right hand!"

"I'm trying!" Kathryn protested.

"Come on!" Andie said hotly. "You want to be an astronaut, you're going to have to master this! Pull on the stick, Kathryn!"

Kathryn spun crazily for a few more seconds. Then Andie threw the switch, and the trainer came to a halt. Kathryn stayed in the chair and shot an angry look over at Andie.

"Why did you stop it?" she said angrily. "I would have had it in another minute."

"On reentry," Andie said quietly, "in another minute, you would have burned up. Come on, out of the chair. We're running late."

Kathryn sat still. "I can do it," she said firmly. "You're not giving me a chance."

Andie looked at her in silence. Once again, she recognized herself only a few years earlier. She knew Kathryn was right.

"Okay," she said. "Five more minutes. Good luck."

She and the others moved on to the next station. Kevin lagged behind the group. Then he ambled over to the training chair.

"Don't let Andie get to you," he said.

Kathryn looked off at the retreating figure of her group leader. "I couldn't please her if I spent the rest of my life trying," she said.

"Maybe," Kevin said, moving closer to her chair. "But why would you want to please anyone except yourself?"

She turned to face him. She looked at him thoughtfully, then asked, "Don't you care about anybody?"

The perfect straight line, Kevin thought. All he had to do now was say — truthfully — "I care about you." But that was a scary thing to do and besides, it wasn't his style. Why should he speak the truth, when a witty remark was available?

"Try me," he said, grinning.

Kathryn looked away. The moment was gone. Kevin turned his thoughts back to the trainer.

"You know," he said, pointing to the control stick, "if you eased up on that thing, you'd be able to handle it. You're trying too hard."

Kathryn looked at him from the corner of her eye. "Then I guess we have something in common," she said.

When she added a smile to the remark, Kevin felt a rush of blood to his head. He smiled back.

"There's a full moon tonight," he said, moving his head a little closer to hers.

"Really?" Kathryn said. "Do you turn into a werewolf?"

He shook his head. "We could check the moon out from the beach."

"Sure," she said. "And get caught breaking curfew. No way."

"If I handle the curfew problem, will you join me?"

"All right," she whispered, staring into his eyes.

"All right!" he said loudly. He leaned toward her, but his elbow accidentally threw the switch on the trainer. As it began to spin, he backed away and watched.

He watched Kathryn spinning, changing directions every few seconds. He saw her moving the control stick back and forth. And after a few seconds, he watched her level out, stabilized and smiling.

Chapter 11

"Are you out of your mind?" Rudy said. "There's no way you're going to get to the beach without getting caught!"

He was sitting on his bunk, surrounded by a ton of classroom notes, diagrams, tables, and other material he had to master before the next day's lecture.

Kevin paced back and forth in front of the bunk, looking at his watch every twenty seconds or so.

"There has to be a way," he mumbled over and over again.

"Besides," Rudy said, "getting caught is only one problem. What do you plan to do about all this stuff we're supposed to read tonight?"

Kevin just continued to pace and mumble. Max came in, stepped around him, and threw himself on his bunk. Right behind him came Tom, one of the technicians who worked on the exhibits at the Space Museum. Tom was trying hard not to lose his temper.

"Max," he said, "if you've got Jinx, turn him over. Otherwise, I'm calling the director."

"What are you," Max said, sitting up, "an Imperial Probe or something?"

Tom looked over at Rudy for a translation. Rudy shrugged. Meanwhile, sensing what was going on, Kevin stepped over to Max's bunk and sat on the footlocker.

"Come on, you guys," Tom said to Rudy and Kevin. "Keep this kid out of trouble. Tell me where he's hiding the robot."

Rudy hunched his shoulders up and pretended to bury himself in his studying. Kevin yawned and stretched his legs out over Max's footlocker.

"Robot?" he said to Tom. "Do you see any robots here? Hey, Rudy, do *you* see any robots? Come on, Tom, we're trying to study."

Tom looked from one boy to another. Then he decided this was a waste of time.

"I guess if he had it in here," he said, "you guys would have seen it. Okay, Max, I'm going. But I'll be keeping an eye on you."

As Tom walked out, Max looked at Kevin, his eyes shining with hero-worship. Kevin got up and opened the footlocker. Inside was Jinx, his domelight off and his arms and legs retracted.

"Well, Jinx," Kevin said, "looks like you have the night off."

He closed the footlocker and looked up to see Max nearly standing at attention in front of him.

"You have saved more than one life today, Han Solo," Max said. "We will not forget."

"Any time, Max," Kevin said distractedly. "Don't mention it."

He went back to his pacing. After only four steps, however, he stopped and looked over at Max.

"Max," Kevin said, "you might be able to help me. You've been coming to SpaceCamp for a couple of years, right?"

"Right," Max answered.

"How do you get to the beach after curfew?"

"Distract and destroy the Imperial Guard," Max said simply.

"Right," Kevin said. "How foolish of me to even ask. Max, be serious! What would you do? What would Luke Skywalker do?"

There was a question Max could answer without hesitation. He did just what Luke would have done. He walked to his locker, opened it, and lifted Jinx out.

"Yo, Jinx," he said.

"Yo, Max," Jinx responded. His domelight began to glow.

"Jinx," Max said, "what's the best way to the beach?"

"Beach," Jinx said. "Go out the main gate. Go to the highway. Turn left."

"Terrific," Kevin said. "That'll take me right past Zach Bergstrom's office."

Max motioned Kevin to be quiet. "Jinx, is there another way to the beach? A *secret* way?"

"Secret," Jinx repeated. "Kept from the knowledge of others. Covert. Stealthy. Furtive — "

"Jinx!" Max groaned. "Just give us another way to the beach!"

Jinx hesitated for only a second. Then he announced, "Turn left before Zach's office. Turn right at Rocket Park. Avoid maintenance building. Go east. Depending on ground speed, beach can be reached between five minutes thirty-seven seconds and twelve minutes fifteen seconds."

Max looked up and smiled at Kevin, who patted him on the back and flew out the door. Rudy watched him go. Then he looked glumly at the books and papers strewn on his bunk.

"I guess pressure doesn't bother him," he said, puzzled.

They sat on the sand listening to the ocean and looking up at the stars. Kevin felt more relaxed than at any other time since he had come to SpaceCamp.

He was being uncharacteristically quiet, because he was enjoying the sound of Kathryn's voice. Right now, she was giving him a tour of the heavens.

"There's the Pleiades, the Seven Sisters, and the Plough," she said, pointing out the sights for him. "It's so beautiful up there. I wish it was like that here."

"You're really into this space stuff, aren't you?" Kevin said, looking over at Kathryn.

"Ever since I was a little kid," she said, still staring at the stars. "My dad used to take me up in his plane. Sometimes at night, I'd try to reach out and touch the stars."

"What's so special about being up there?" he asked.

"It seems like anything is possible in space," she said, looking at him. "We could do things right. Not mess it up, the way we have down here."

"But how can you get so worked up about something like that?" he asked. "We're all going to be wiped out by the bomb, anyway."

"That's a cop-out, Kevin," she said, looking out over the ocean. "That's an excuse for people who are afraid to try."

"I'm not afraid," he said. "I just don't care, that's all."

"Oh, yes, you do," she said softly, looking at him again. "It's just easier to say you don't care. You think it's too risky to admit that something is important to you."

They both looked out at the ocean. Then

55

Kathryn added, "And it *is* risky. But you have to do it, anyway."

"I'll never tell!" Max growled, as he sat on his bunk. "Torture me. Kill me, if you like. But I'll never tell!"

Rudy watched the proceedings from his own bunk. He had pretended to be asleep when word reached the room that Andie was on her way.

"Nobody is going to torture you, Max," Andie said. "But we will find out where they are."

Zach came in, wearing a raincoat over his pajamas. "What is it?" he asked Andie.

"Kathryn and Kevin aren't in their bunks," she said.

Zach looked around the room at the sleepy faces. "Okay, let's have it," he said. "Where are they?"

As he said it, Jinx came wheeling out of the bathroom.

"Kevin and Kathryn went to the beach," Jinx said. "It's a secret."

"Oooooh, Jinx!" Max cried.

"Oooooh, Max!" Jinx squealed in imitation.

Chapter 12

The van pulled up to the paths leading to the dorm entrances. Andie and Zach got out of the front seat, Kathryn and Kevin out of the back.

Without a word, Zach led Kevin to his dorm. Equally as silent, Kathryn marched single file behind Andie. Halfway to the dorm, Andie slowed to allow Kathryn to catch up with her.

"I expected more from you, Kathryn," she said.

"We were just talking."

"That's not the point," Andie said heatedly, "and you know it."

Kathryn stopped walking and faced Andie. "All I know," she said, "is that you've been ragging me since day one. Will you tell me why?"

Surprised at the emotion, Andie hesitated a few seconds. Then she said, "Because you're special. I knew it the first time I saw you."

"Knew what?" Kathryn asked, softening her tone.

"I saw the look in your eyes," Andie said. "It was like looking in a mirror. A long time ago, John Glenn winked at me. And I came running."

Now Kathryn was the one to show surprise. After a pause, she asked, "Then why are you so hard on me?"

"Like I said, you're special," Andie answered. "You're going to get up there. And when it's your turn, you'll have the drill down better than anyone else. Every 'i' will be dotted. Every 't' will be crossed. That's how I learned it. That's how you'll learn it."

She gave the message some seconds to sink in. Then she broke the silence with a Mission Control request for affirmation.

"Do you copy, Kathryn?"

"I copy," Kathryn said softly.

"Good. Now go inside and get to bed."

Zach's speech to Kevin was considerably less friendly, and Kevin let that be known by the way he burst into the dorm.

"Who told?" he bellowed.

Max jumped out of his bunk and said, "It wasn't me, Han Solo! The Emperor got the information out of Jinx!"

Kevin had finally had enough of the *Star Wars* game. "Max," he said angrily, "I'm not Han Solo! And you're not Luke Skywalker, and there is no Empire, no Death Star, and no Force.

You're just an ordinary kid, and so am I, for that matter! And maybe nobody lives happily ever after! So just stay away from me! Stay *far* away!"

Kevin threw himself on his bunk and buried his face in the pillow. Max stood looking at the back of his hero, the hero who only a few hours earlier had patted him on the back for a job well done.

Afraid he was going to burst into tears, Max ran from the room, down the hall, and into the bathroom. Jinx, hidden under a sink, rolled out when Max came in.

Max sat on the floor in a corner and held his head in his hands.

"I wish I *was* far away!" he said, sobbing. "I wish I was anywhere except here. I wish I was in *space*!"

Jinx stood there, taking it all in. When Max finished talking to himself, Jinx hesitated a second, then turned and rolled down the hall and out of the building.

He left the campgrounds and moved down the road toward the NASA complex. When he reached the locked gate, Jinx punched in a code, and the gate swung open.

A security guard stepped out of a booth to see who was entering. "Hey, Jinx," he called.

A scientific dissertation on hay crossed Jinx's circuits, but he had more important things to do. He rolled past the booth and made his way

to a nearby building. Inside the building, he
went straight for the computer room.

Jinx stood before a screen attached to the
main bank of NASA computers. He extended
an arm and plugged it into an outlet next to
the computer's keyboard. The computer spoke
to Jinx in a flat, unmusical version of Jinx's
voice.

"Enter authorization code," it said.

"MP-16347-JX," Jinx responded.

After a few seconds, the computer said,
"Hello, Jinx. How can NASA help you?"

"Put Max Graham in space," Jinx said.

Another pause. Then the computer said,
"There is no Max Graham listed in the astronaut program."

Jinx brought his other arm to the keyboard
and pressed some buttons.

"There is now," he said.

Chapter 13

Andie and the other team leaders, each wearing a radio headset, lined the side of the pool, watching their teams working underwater. Each team was working on a separate section of a space station model on the floor of the pool.

The crew members all wore space suits, including helmets with radio headsets, and they all moved in slow motion. It was only an illusion, as though they were all involved in making a movie about building a space station.

Andie was not happy as she watched her team behaving very unlike a team. Tish and Kathryn each held one side of a solar panel section, as they waited for Rudy to decipher the instructions and let them know how to insert the section.

Andie was monitoring the conversation, which was building into an argument.

"Rudy," Kathryn said, "would you make up your mind? Is it 37A first, or 39B?"

"I think it's 37A," Rudy said, trying to read the diagram on the plastic page he held in front of his visor. "It's hard to think when you're weightless."

"You mean when you're witless," Tish said. "It's 39B first. I remember seeing it in the book."

"No," Rudy said with very little confidence. I'm pretty sure it's 37A."

Andie watched Kevin float down to join the others. Then she listened to him talk to them.

"Rudy, you were supposed to study that diagram *before* we got here," he said.

"Come on, Rudy," Tish said, "like, the whole world is waiting, you know what I mean?"

"Yeah?" Rudy said, exasperated. "Well, you're the one with the photographic memory, Ambrose. You do it."

He flung the diagram, and it floated slowly toward Tish. She let go of her end of the panel and reached for the page. As the panel began floating upward, Kathryn tried to pull it down.

"I can't hold it!" Kathryn cried.

"Then let go!" Kevin said.

Kathryn let the panel slip from her hands. It floated up, hit the two panels already in place, and knocked them loose. All three panels floated to the surface of the water.

"I don't believe this!" Kevin said.

"Nobody would believe this!" Andie said into her headset from poolside. "The solar panels on the *real* space station went up faster than yours! Is this what you people mean by teamwork?"

She looked over at Max, sitting on the edge of the pool in shorts and a T-shirt. "Come on, Max," she said, "go get a suit and show these guys how it's done."

"No, thanks," Max said gloomily. "They don't want me around."

Andie sighed and turned back to watch her crew trying to get their panels back into place. Jinx moved up behind her, rolled past her, and stopped behind Max. He extended an arm and pushed Max into the water.

Rolling away, Jinx said, "Practice, practice, Max. The big day is coming."

"What's wrong, honey?" Zach asked. They had just finished dinner, and Andie hadn't said a full sentence since they'd met in the parking lot to come home.

"I don't know," she said, slumping down on the couch. "I guess I'm just not very good at being a counselor."

"Sure you are, Andie."

"I don't even want to be good at it!" she protested. "I'm an astronaut. *That's* my job! Except NASA doesn't seem to agree. I don't know, Zach, all the work I've done, and I'm just a glorified baby-sitter."

"Andie," he said, trying to soothe her, "things don't always happen the way we think they should. Keep working with the kids. Look at it as part of your own training."

"Maybe I should quit the space program. Get a job as a waitress. Except I'd probably spill soup all over everyone."

"Honey," Zach said, "I know you're impatient. But it's worth waiting for — getting into space."

There was a kind of sadness in his voice that caught her attention. She sat up and looked at him.

"I thought you didn't think about going back up again," she said.

"I can't go up again," Zach said. "But even when you're actually up there, it feels like — like a memory. As though you aren't really there. It's almost as though you're looking at pictures — the pictures you've been seeing all your life."

"Zach — " Andie said.

"Yeah," Zach sighed. "I think about it. I think about it every single day."

She stood and walked over to him. She put her arms around his neck and kissed him lightly on the cheek.

"The kids really are part of it, Andie," he said, smiling at her.

"I know that, Zach. I know it."

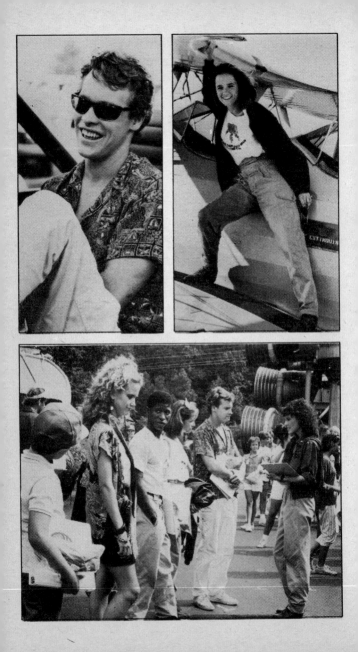

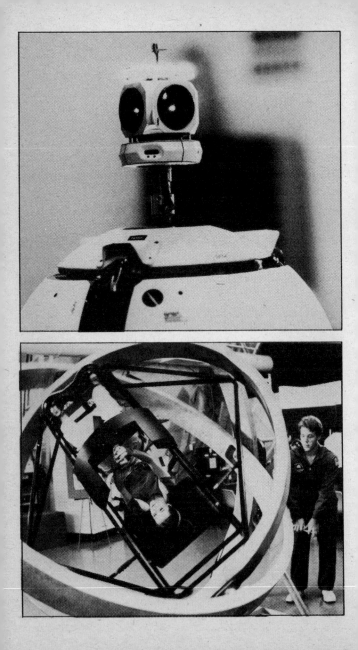

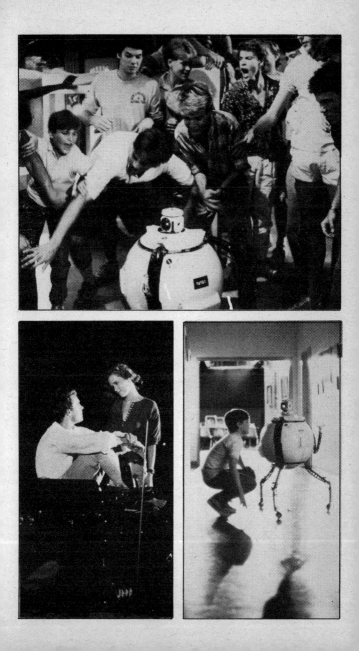

Chapter 14

The notice on the bulletin board read:

THURSDAY, 3:30 PM.
BLUE AND GREEN TEAMS.
SHUTTLE FRF.
LAUNCH PAD 77A

Kathryn, Tish, and two members of the green team stood reading it as Zach came out of his office.

"Tomorrow afternoon!" Kathryn said.

"Zach," Tish called, "what's FRF?"

"Flight Readiness Firing," Zach said. "That's how NASA tests the main engines on the shuttle."

"You mean you're going to test those two rockets that are on either side of the shuttle on the launch pad?" asked Tish.

"No," said Zach. "Those are the Solid Rocket Boosters. If we turned those on, the shuttle would launch. They provide most of the power to lift the shuttle off the launch pad and propel it during the first two minutes of flight. They use up all their fuel in about two minutes, and then they float down to the ocean by parachute and are reused. No, what we test during the Flight Readiness Firing is the shuttle's main engines. Those are the three large nozzles you see on the base of the shuttle itself. They assist the Solid Rocket Boosters during takeoff and help the shuttle gain speed and altitude after the Solid Rocket Boosters have separated. The main engines are fed by the giant external fuel tank that the shuttle is attached to. After the tank's fuel is gone, the main engines shut off, and the tank drops to the ocean and disintegrates. From then on, the shuttle is powered by the two smaller OMS — Orbital Maneuvering System — engines located next to the main engines. In fact, when the shuttle returns to Earth, it glides. The landing is done without power."

Tish's eyes had begun to glaze over from the long list of facts.

"This is the first year we have permission for campers to experience an FRF," continued Zach. "Some of you will even sit in the shuttle when we test the main engines and get an astronaut's view."

"Sounds like, you know, real exciting?" said Tish, unconvinced.

Jinx rolled by, lights flashing. "Real exciting," he said. And he took off for the library to learn all he could about Flight Readiness Firing.

Late that afternoon, four members of the green team sat at the console in the Mission Control mock-up. Among the things they watched on the console were video monitors showing the blue team inside the shuttle simulator. Kevin and Kathryn sat up front on the flight deck, in position as commander and pilot. Rudy was behind them in the aft crew station preparing to operate the controls for the Remote Manipulator System that would send Max out of the shuttle simulator to recover a model of a satellite.

Tish and Max were on the mid-deck, the deck below the flight deck that held the eating, sleeping, and hygiene areas. Tish stood at the air lock, ready to open it for the trip Max was about to take. And Max stood near her, wearing his tiny space suit, which made him look like an inflatable toy.

Andie and Zach stood behind the green team in Mission Control, each with a clipboard, both eager to get the proceedings started. They listened through headsets as Kevin and Kathryn went through the last-minute check.

"Range scale at orbit on primary," said Kevin.

"Roger, secondary," answered Kathryn.

"Enter OMS-1 burn program, pilot."

"Roger, OMS-1."

"Stand by, pilot."

Then Banning, the green team launch director, spoke to them. "Atlantis, this is control. We have orbit confirmed, 125 nautical miles, inclination 35 degrees. You are in position for satellite recovery."

This message sent Tish into action. She removed her sunglasses and her earrings and put them on a table. Then she opened the air lock entry hatch to allow Max to enter.

"Roger, Control," Tish said. "Air lock open. Activating cargo bay doors."

Max moved slowly, as a walking inflatable toy might be expected to move. He left the air lock and entered the huge cargo bay, the area in which the shuttle carried its many different payloads. The shuttle was, after all, a sort of space truck. Its main function was to carry cargo, not people, into space.

As Max watched the giant cargo bay doors open above him, he lifted himself onto the RMS arm that would soon extend outside the ship in the direction of the satellite.

"How come I have to do all the dangerous stuff?" he mumbled into his microphone.

"Come on, Max," Kathryn's voice responded. "Dale Gardner and Joe Allen did this on Discovery 51A."

To that, Kevin's voice answered, "I don't think that's going to make him feel better."

Max was now strapped securely onto the RMS

arm in the cargo bay. Tish moved to her next post, and Max gestured that he was ready.

"You're on, Rudy," Kevin said.

Rudy went to work on the controls. Max began to move away from the side of the ship, attached to the RMS arm that would extend as far as the satellite that Max was going to recover.

At Mission Control, the wide-eyed green team watched the action on their screens. From inside the shuttle, just as wide-eyed, Kathryn, Tish, and Kevin watched Max glide toward the satellite.

The gliding came to an abrupt end when Rudy banged an elbow on the control panel. He reached to grab the pained area and knocked over his clipboard. By the time he bent down to pick up the clipboard, Max was screaming into everyone's headset.

"Rudeeeee! What are you doing to me?!"

Instead of gliding, Max was now bouncing along the same path. The RMS arm hit bottom, then flew ten feet into the air, hit bottom, flew ten feet into the air, down, up, down, up —

In Mission Control, the green team was enjoying the show immensely. Grinning at his fellow team members, Banning said into his mike, "Instigate emergency power loss scenario."

"Yes, sir," Gardener responded. "Killing power."

That put a stop to Max's bouncing. Unfortunately, the remote manipulator arm was at its highest point when the power died, and Max now found himself looking down at the ship.

"Get me down from here!" he screamed into his mike. "I'm gonna be sick!"

"Control," Kathryn said, "this is Atlantis. We're experiencing electrical failure in the RMS. Switching to auxiliary cells."

"That's my decision," Kevin said, "not yours."

"Then why didn't you make it?" she snapped.

Rudy was on his knees, peering into the electrical panel under the control board. He looked from the wiring to his diagram, back and forth, back and forth.

"Here we go again, you know?" Tish said, looking down at him. "Rudy, it's the thick cable?"

"I know what I'm doing," Rudy said uncertainly. "It's the green one next to the red one — there!"

And the lights went out. Kathryn screamed into her mike, "Rudy, what are you doing?"

Rudy tried another connection, and a series of sirens and horns began wailing. Up front, Kathryn decided that she had had enough. She bolted from her chair and marched to the rear.

"Hey!" Kevin called after her. "Sit down! That's an order!"

Kathryn ignored him, reached the control panel, and pushed herself between Tish and Rudy.

"Kathryn!" Tish cried. "That's Rudy's job!"

"Get out of there, Kathryn!" Rudy said. " I can do it."

The green team was now laughing hysterically. They, together with Andie and Zach, listened to the sirens and the horns — and to the scuffle taking place underneath the control panel.

"What's going on in there?" Andie demanded. "We're showing a second OMS burn!"

Kevin's voice shouted over the noise, "Pilot must have hit the switch when she got up."

"Why isn't she at her post?" Andie asked.

Kevin looked back at the mess going on near the control panel. "She's too busy doing everyone else's job," he responded.

"Shuttle," Banning said, laughing, "you're falling out of orbit."

"Take over, commander!" Andie said.

"Hey," Kevin said coolly, "it's not my job, man. Talk to the pilot."

"Orbit is decaying, Atlantis," Banning said. "You're coming up on atmospheric interface. You're gonna be toast."

"Pilot!" Andie yelled. "Do you copy! Pilot!"

"I'm sorry," Kevin said in his best answering machine imitation, "but Kathryn can't come to the phone right now. If you leave a message after the tone — "

"Atlantis," Banning said, "you're coming up on interface."

"Roger, Control," Kevin said chuckling. He

turned to face the crew, just as Kathryn made the connection to turn off the alarms.

"Ladies and gentlemen," Kevin said, grinning, "please return your seats and tray tables to their full upright position and extinguish all smoking materials. We hope you've enjoyed your flight with Atlantis Airlines — "

He stopped cold when the hatch door slammed open and Andie stepped inside.

"Stop it!" she cried. "Stop it, all of you!"

She stood there panting in anger, and her breath was the only sound that could be heard for several seconds. The silence was broken by Max's voice.

"Somebody get me down from here!" he pleaded.

"Kathryn left her post," Tish said.

"I'm sorry," Kathryn said, straightening out her coveralls to keep from looking at Andie. "Rudy couldn't fix it, and I knew how to — "

"SHUT UP!" Andie commanded.

She looked each of them over icily. Then, her voice much calmer, she said, "I don't want to hear it. I *can't* hear it. Do you know why? Because you're all *dead*!"

"Oh, come on, Andie," Kevin said.

She turned a fierce glare on him. "You just disintegrated during reentry. Don't you know what that means? You're all dead because you couldn't work as a team! And *you*, Mr. Donaldson, are responsible."

"*Me?*" he said, genuinely shocked.

"*You!* You're shuttle commander. You're responsible for everything that happens on this ship."

"Really," he said angrily. "Well, just remember that I didn't ask to be responsible!"

"And that," Andie said in disbelief, "is your excuse for killing four people?"

"I don't believe this," Kevin laughed. "Nobody got killed, Andie. I mean, hey, this is only SpaceCamp!"

Chapter 15

To Kevin, it was only SpaceCamp. To Jinx, however, it was the opportunity to return a lifesaving favor. Ever since he had heard Max's plea — "I wish I was in space" — Jinx had devoted himself to giving his friend what he wanted.

He was now hooked into the main computer, trying to learn how to use the FRF training to help Max get into space. He asked the computer to go over launch possibilities with him.

JINX: With Max in shuttle during Flight Readiness Firing, what is worst possible thing that could happen?

COMPUTER: Worst case scenario 310437. Thermal Curtain Failure.

JINX: Define Thermal Curtain Failure.

COMPUTER: Failure of the heat shield during main engine test. One Solid Rocket Booster will overheat and ignite. Result — shuttle will be forced to launch.

JINX: Will launch be successful?

The computer answered with a graphic animation on its screen. It showed a drawing of the shuttle, with one Solid Rocket Booster blinking. The shuttle rose from the ground. Then it flipped over and crashed.

COMPUTER: A shuttle launched with only one Solid Rocket Booster ignited will turn like a pinwheel and crash. To avoid worst case scenario, second Solid Rocket Booster must be ignited. Result — a perfect launch.

Now the computer showed another graphic drawing. This drawing had two boosters blinking. The shuttle rose and took off in a perfect launch.

JINX: Thermal Curtain Failure possibilities?
COMPUTER: NASA estimate. Probability of one Thermal Curtain Failure every 4.9 million years.

JINX: Too long for Max to wait.

Jinx removed his arm from the computer terminal and rolled toward the exit. "Thermal Curtain Failure," his speaker said. "Piece of cake."

Chapter 16

Early the next morning, Andie stood outside the dorm, pacing near the door. Kevin, Tish, and Kathryn waited inside a shuttle bus that would take the team to the launch site.

"Will you guys get a move on?" Andie called.

No sooner had she said it than Rudy came charging out of the building. He bounded toward the bus, tripped himself, began to lose his balance, then regained it just before hitting his knee on the edge of the bus door.

Andie watched him stumble aboard the bus. Then she turned to see Max leave the building, loudly whistling the theme music from *Star Wars*. She followed Max to the bus and stepped inside after he had marched aboard.

Later that day, Andie and the rest of the team marched to the open-air elevator that would lift them to the shuttle. Each member wore NASA coveralls and carried a helmet. When they reached the elevator shaft, Andie brought them a step closer to the real astronauts by handing out headsets.

"These are short-range," she said. "They wouldn't work on a real flight, but you'll be able to use them to talk to Control. And remember. . . ."

The blue team sang out in unison, "Don't touch anything!"

The elevator arrived, and they all watched as the members of the purple team filed out. They had the flushed look of people who had just taken the most exciting roller coaster ride of their lives.

"Wait till you see it!" the first girl said.

"What a rush!" said the second girl out of the elevator. "There's nothing like it!"

"Totally awesome!" a boy said.

Then a second boy followed him out. His face was the color of a dollar bill, and he was staggering as he stepped off the elevator. As his team leader helped him down the ramp, Andie led her own crew into the elevator, closed the door, and pushed a button. As they rose from the ground, Jinx turned a corner and watched. Max saw him below and waved to him.

"Hello, Max," Jinx said, though no one was close enough to hear him.

He turned and began rolling away, since he had business to take care of in the computer room. "Good-bye, Max," he said. "I hope you enjoy space."

Chapter 17

Once Kevin and Kathryn were strapped into the commander's and pilot's seats, Andie showed Max, Tish, and Rudy where to position themselves on the flight deck and mid-deck of the shuttle.

"Please put on your helmets," Andie said. Then, facing front, she added, "Pilot and commander, prepare for Flight Readiness Firing."

Kathryn and Kevin scanned the controls in front of them, as Andie spoke into her headset mike.

"Control, this is the Space Shuttle Atlantis. Do you copy?"

With Zach standing over his shoulder reading the screen output, the launch director answered, "Roger, Atlantis, this is Launch Control confirming radio check."

In the shuttle, the members of the blue team exchanged grins, as the Launch Control response came in over their headsets. The next message followed close behind. "Solid Rocket Boosters A and B ignition off. Stand by for main engine test. Atlantis, do you copy?"

Kevin looked over at Kathryn and saw the excitement in her eyes. 'Go ahead," he said. "Answer the man."

"You mean it?" she asked.

He smiled at her and nodded.

"Roger, Control," she said into the mike. "Check is satisfactory. Over." Then she looked at Kevin and beamed. "All right!" she cried.

Back in Mission Control, everything was calm as the technicians prepared to test the shuttle's main engines. It was just routine.

Two buildings away, however, a funny-looking robot was preparing to turn the routine into an earth-shattering event. Jinx stood at the computer terminal that had given him the information he needed to grant Max's wish. Now, as countdown for the engine testing began, Jinx stood ready.

"Stand by for FRF ignition." The crew listened to the message from Control through their headsets. "T minus ten, nine, eight, seven, six, five, four, three, two, one. . . ."

A switch was thrown in the control room. The shuttle began to vibrate. A deep rumble grew into a roar. Through the windows, the crew could see nothing but steam.

"We have main engine start," they heard Control say.

Kathryn and Kevin exchanged grins, Rudy let out a whoop, and Tish stared at a window with her mouth gaping open. Only Max seemed to be having something less than the time of his life. He sat staring straight ahead, his hands tightly grasping the armrests of his chair.

Jinx was now hooked into the main computer, watching its screen for reports of progress of the shuttle test firing. As the test progressed, he entered his own information into the system, all of it based on what he had learned about Thermal Curtain Failure.

"Looking good," the crew heard Control say. "Main engines at one hundred percent."

"Test termination at T plus twenty-five seconds," another voice said. "Now at T plus twelve, thirteen. . . ."

Jinx listened and watched the dots on the screen change color. "T plus fifteen," the voice said, "sixteen, seventeen. . . ." Then Jinx flicked a switch.

The technicians were going through their routines, just as they did every time there was a test firing. The kids on board were shouting with delight. They were slapping palms with one another, when suddenly alarms went off both in the control room and in the shuttle.

"We have overheat on Booster B!" an excited voice said.

"Terminate the test!" the launch director ordered.

Chapter 18

"The thermal curtain!" a technician yelled. "It's failing!"

"Terminate!" Zach called out from behind the director. "Terminate!"

"Thermal curtain has failed!" the technician announced. "We have Thermal Curtain Failure!"

"Booster B temperature is rising," another voice said. "Booster B temperature is critical. It's going to light!"

Inside the shuttle, Andie struggled to get Kathryn unstrapped from her seat.

"Make 'em stop!" Rudy screeched. "Make 'em turn it off!"

"They're trying!" Andie replied, as she helped Kathryn down from her seat.

"We're past shutdown temperature!" they heard a voice say. "We can't stop it! Booster B is near ignition! It's lit!"

Andie was now strapping herself into Kathryn's seat. "Light Booster A!" she screamed into her headset. "Light it and launch us or we'll explode!"

"She's right!" Zach screamed, back at Control. "Ignite Booster A! Do it or they'll all be dead!"

After a second's hesitation, the launch director said, "Ignite Booster A!"

The already deafening roar increased in intensity. Max and Tish covered their ears. Andie sat in the pilot's seat throwing switches and pushing buttons. The crew watched as though they were in a trance.

For a moment, the shuttle sat on the launch pad, waiting like a great eagle gathering the courage to break free from its cage. Then, the crew access arm moved back and slowly the shuttle began to rise. Inside, the crew was plastered into their seats by the force. Kathryn, who hadn't had time to strap back in, was wedged against the bulkhead, held in place by Rudy.

Proudly, majestically, the shuttle rose above the smoke and flames created by its engines.

"It worked!" Zach cried, staring at the computer screen. "We have lift-off!"

In the main computer room, Jinx watched the same scene. " 'Bye, Max," he said.

Chapter 19

"Roll maneuver complete, Atlantis," the launch director said, as Zach watched over his shoulder. "You're looking good." He looked up at Zach and asked, "You want to take it from here?"

"Thanks," Zach said. He took the mike, paused for a second, then said, "Andie. . . ."

"Guess I won't have to wait so long, after all," she said over the headseat without a trace of humor in her voice.

"I guess not," he said. "Andie, you're going to have to throttle."

"Copy, Control," she said. "Main engines at sixty-five percent."

Andie took a quick look around her and saw that her crew was shaking with fear as well as the force of the lift-off. "Hang on," she told them. "You're experiencing three G's. That's three times the force of gravity. I know it's tough. . . ."

She spoke to Kevin in the seat beside her. "We have to drop the Solid Rocket Boosters. They're on your side. Now, arm the separators."

Kevin turned a panicked look at her. "I don't know which ones!" he pleaded.

"The left ones!" Andie shouted. "The whole bank!"

"Atlantis," Zach's voice said, "you are go for Solid Rocket Booster separation."

"Hit them!" Andie screamed at Kevin. "Hit them!"

Kevin did as he was told. "Control," Andie said more calmly, "this is Atlantis. We have SRB separation. Over."

"Atlantis, this is Control," Zach said. "Press for Main Engine Cut-Off. Repeat, you are go for MECO, over." Then, in a less mechanical voice, he added, "I don't know where this drill is going to end, honey. But hang in there."

"Roger — " they heard. Then static, and finally silence.

"We're losing her!" Zach said in panic.

"The bird wasn't flight-ready, Zach," the launch director said, trying to calm him. "They only have short-range radio."

Andie tore off her headset, which was useless now. "Kevin," she said, "we have MECO. Go for external tank separation. Hit the third switch on the left, on my mark. Three, two, one, *mark!*"

"Got it," Kevin said, hitting the switch.

Through the windows, the crew saw a flash. Kevin had separated the external tank from the shuttle. The tank sailed away, and the shuttle continued on.

Zach stared at the monitor. "They're still climbing," he said. "Come on, Andie!"

"Sir," one of the other technicians said, speaking to the director. "We have a track on Atlantis. It shows that they're at one-eighty by . . . by thirty-three! They're in orbit!"

For the first time, Zach became aware of how many people had come into the building. The technician's announcement brought a huge cheer from the control team and from several dozen onlookers, who were monitoring the chain of events as nervously as Zach himself.

They're in orbit, Zach thought. Well, that's good news and bad news.

Chapter 20

Inside the shuttle, the crew sat in near silence, frozen in position. For a long time, only the hum of the cooling system could be heard as they sailed in orbit around Earth.

Rudy broke the silence in a soft, shaky voice. "I didn't touch a thing, Andie," he said.

"I know," Andie said, unbuckling her seat belt. "Even you wouldn't have been able to cause this, Rudy."

She had her belt undone, and she held onto the arms of her seat. "Well, ladies and gentlemen," she said, as cheerily as she could, "we seem to have achieved orbit. Doesn't that call for some sort of celebration?"

She let go of her armrests and floated up from her seat. The kids looked at her in awe.

"She's floating!" Kevin gasped.

"Very perceptive of you, Kevin," Andie said. She floated over to Kathryn.

"You okay?" she asked, as Kathryn floated up beside her.

Smiling giddily, Kathryn said, "I could have done without the lift-off. But this is unreal!"

Rudy released himself from his seat the same time Kevin did. They floated upward and began doing a series of midair flips in slow motion.

"We're weightless!" Rudy screeched. "I mean zero-gravity! All right!"

Floating up beside Kathryn, Kevin asked, "May I have the next dance?"

Andie looked down at the two remaining crew members, both still harnessed into their seats.

"Tish?" she called. "Max? Are you okay?"

Tish sat with her hands on her enormous hanging earrings, which were not hanging, but standing upright above her ears.

"People are floating in front of me!" she groaned. "I thought I was going to die, and now here I am in another dimension! Oh, I feel sick!"

Andie floated down to soothe her. At the same time, Rudy glided over to Max, who sat frowning, with his eyes closed and his hands over his ears.

"Max, old boy?" Rudy said softly, putting his hand on Max's shoulder.

Max opened his eyes and looked around. "I want to go home," he said.

"We will go home, man," Rudy said, smiling. "But first, you have to try this flying."

"Not right now," Max said.

Kevin, floating by Tish, said, "Love your earrings." Tish glared at him and began undoing her seat belt.

"Everybody seems to be in one piece," Andie said, climbing back into her seat and slipping her feet under the restraining straps. "Let's discuss the situation."

"Look!" Kathryn cried. She pointed out the aft window. Kevin, Rudy, and Tish floated over to see. Kathryn's voice was strong enough even to lure Max from his seat.

They all floated to the window and shared the sight with Kathryn. Pure white light, like nothing they had ever seen before, began to steal across their faces.

"Wow!" Tish whispered. "Like, cosmic!"

Andie released herself from her chair and floated over to join them. They were getting an unfamiliar view of a sphere they all knew well.

"Wow!" Max exclaimed. "That's Earth!"

"Look!" Kevin shouted, pointing. "There's Mexico!"

"And America!" Kathryn said. "Hey, there's Florida!"

While they all gaped, Kevin moved next to Kathryn and whispered softly in her ear. "Maybe you could touch those stars now," he said.

"Yeah," she said, staring out. "It sure feels like I could."

"Andie," Max whined, bringing them all back to reality, "I want to go *home!*"

Andie pushed herself away from the window and floated back to her seat. "We're going home, Max," she said, speaking to the whole group. "But you're all going to have to help."

One by one, the crew members pushed away from the window and turned to face her. Andie wasn't surprised to see that Kathryn was the last to make the move.

Andie sat in the pilot's seat and wedged her feet back into the restraints. She entered the date into the computer console in front of her.

"We have no contact with NASA," she reminded the crew. "But they can still read our instruments. So I'm sure they're planning right now to bring us down on automatic, at the next available window."

"Window?" Max asked. "What kind of window?"

"A window," Andie explained, "is one of the places where we can reenter Earth's atmosphere. We need to determine the coordinates and exact time of reentry so that we can land at Edwards Air Force Base."

All of this seemed to relax the crew. It helped to know that something was possible, and that it was being done.

"So what do we do now?" Tish asked.

"We just sit tight and keep everything running," Andie answered. "We should be at the first window for Edwards in twelve hours."

She turned back to the computer keyboard and began entering data. Tish looked at Kathryn, who looked at Kevin, who looked at Rudy, who looked at Max. Then they went back to their seats to wait.

Back at Launch Control, Zach was busy reading the board. Marty Brennan, in charge of NASA public relations, spoke angrily to the back of Zach's head.

"Keep a lid on it?" Brennan wailed. "Just how do you propose I do that, Zach? People five hundred miles away know the shuttle went up!"

"Tell them the truth, Marty," Zach said, without looking away from the board. "Tell them we just launched my wife and five SpaceCamp kids by mistake." He turned to look up at Brennan. "Don't worry. No one will ever believe it."

"But the White House has to be told, too!" Brennan protested.

"Marty," Zach said, turning back to the board, "they'll be back in twelve hours!"

"Zach," said one of the technicians, as he came up behind him, "we have to find an earlier reentry point."

"Why?" Zach asked, looking worried.

"The shuttle wasn't flight-ready," the technician said. "It's the oxygen. There isn't enough to last twelve hours."

Chapter 21

The oxygen question had, of course, occurred to Andie. However, she didn't want to bring it up until the crew had had a chance to savor the wonder of being in space. When they had had their chance, she broke the bad news.

Now, Andie and Kevin were studying a computer screen that graphically outlined the situation for them. OXYGEN, it said across the top of the screen. Below that, there were ten columns. The first nine flashed large zeros. The last column flashed a message: 98%.

"How long will one tank last?" Kevin asked nervously.

"Twelve hours," Andie said.

"Terrific!" Kevin said. "Then we're okay!"

"Afraid not," Andie said. "We'll need more for reentry. At least another hour, probably two."

A few minutes later, she explained the situation to the group. "Okay," she concluded, "so no oxygen was provided for the life support system. That's where we are. Where do we go from here?"

Silence. Then Rudy sat up, his eyes widening. "What about the propulsion system for the OMS engines?" he said excitedly. "We can raid the liquid oxygen from there!"

"No good," Kathryn said quietly. "The propulsion system uses nitrogen tetroxide. We want to breathe, not dry-clean our clothes."

"We have to think," Andie said, shaking her head. "Where can we get oxygen?"

"I could run down to the 7–Eleven," Kevin said with his usual grin.

Andie stared blankly at him. Then her eyes lit up. "I've got it!" she cried.

She turned to the computer keyboard and rapidly typed in a program. The crew members exchanged puzzled glances, then huddled around to look over Andie's shoulder.

Tish decided to break the silence. "Er, like, you want to share this with us, Andie?" she asked.

"Sure," Andie said, busily typing. "We're going to Daedalus."

"The space station!" Kathryn said, smiling. "Of course! They have oxygen storage!"

"All of you get back to your stations," Andie said, as she finished entering her program. "Rudy and Kathryn, unstow the deck seats.

Prepare for roll. I just hope we can make it in time."

The launch director had taken over, and Zach was pacing back and forth behind him. He glanced at the board every now and then, but mostly stared at his moving feet.

"If we could only talk to her," he said in frustration. "Just to remind her about Daedalus!"

"Zach," the launch director said soothingly, "she's a good pilot. She'll think of it."

"Yeah," Zach said thoughtfully. "You're right. Still, if we could only talk to her for a minute...."

"We're going for Daedalus interface," Andie said into her headset. She was in the pilot seat, and she looked over at Kevin in his commander's position.

"Roger," Kevin said into his headset. "Power up."

"Give me a course bearing," Andie said. She looked over at Kevin, who was running his eyes back and forth across the instrument panel. "Come on, Kevin," Andie said impatiently. "You did this in the simulator!"

After a pause, Kevin answered, "I faked it."

"Out of the seat," Andie said immediately. "Kathryn, move up here."

She looked sharply over at Kevin, who had

not yet made a move. "Out!" she commanded.

Kathryn unbuckled herself from one of the mid-deck seats and switched places with Kevin.

"Course bearing," Andie said.

"Oh-niner-five-five-niner," Kathryn answered smartly.

"Stand by for OMS burn," Andie said. "Go for OMS!"

At Mission Control, there was a burst of spontaneous applause as the "blip" that represented the shuttle Atlantis on the big board suddenly arced upward to a higher orbit.

"She remembered!" Zach cried, when it was clear the ship was heading for Daedalus. "You were absolutely right!" he said, slapping the launch director on the back. "She is a good pilot. One of the best!"

Then, looking at the monitor, he said softly, "Prove us right, baby. Please prove us right."

In the computer room, Jinx was once again plugged into the main computer. Soft, short beeps came from his speakers, as he studied the screen that told of the condition of the shuttle flight.

"Oxygen supply," he requested.

"Time until landing," the computer responded, "fourteen hours. Estimated oxygen supply, 11 hours 56 minutes."

"Max will . . . erase?" Jinx asked.

"Probability one hundred percent," the computer answered.

"Get Max out of space now," Jinx said. "How?"

"NASA is working on the problem," the computer said.

Jinx quickly pulled his arm from the computer terminal. He turned and rolled toward the exit.

"NASA needs help," he said loudly.

Chapter 22

It took over eleven hours to reach the space station.

"Give me a Daedalus ETA," Andie said from the commander's seat.

From the pilot's seat, Kathryn answered, "Estimated time of arrival at Daedalus, twenty-six minutes."

Andie read several instruments, flipped a few switches, then sat back and turned toward the pilot's seat. "I'm glad you're here, Kathryn," she said.

Surprised, Kathryn looked over at her. Then she smiled weakly and said, "I'm glad *you're* here."

The rest of the crew was working on the mid-deck, busily examining the storage lockers to see what supplies had been put onto the ship.

"Tish," Kevin said, floating up to her, "did you find anything?"

"Not much," Tish answered. "Just two suits

in the air lock and some rope. How did Rudy make out with the food?"

"Lemonade drink," Rudy said, floating over. "Also strawberry drink, orange drink, and pineapple drink."

"We sure won't get thirsty," Max said from his seat. They all exchanged glum looks.

Twenty minutes later, Tish, Rudy, Kevin, and Max watched from their seats as the space station grew larger and larger. It was still far enough away to look like a box kite, but everyone on board knew that it contained their only hope for survival.

"Andie," Kathryn asked, reading the control panel, "how do we go through reentry without help from Ground Control?"

"I'll handle it, Kathryn," Andie said quietly. Kathryn — and everyone else — could tell from her voice that Andie wasn't at all sure that she could handle it.

"I had an idea about that," Tish said, floating through the crew hatch from the mid-deck. "Andie, you know how you said like they have that telemetry stuff? Like they could read all our instruments? Well, I was thinking — or maybe I was just inspired — you know, with the view and all. . . ."

"Tish," Andie said impatiently, "*what* idea?"

"Oh, yeah. Code. Using the CXT switch? You know, *code*."

"Code!" Andie said, brightening. "Tish, that's

a great idea! You mean Morse code? Terrific! Does anybody here know Morse code?"

"Me," Tish said lightly.

Andie stared at her for a few seconds. "You? You know Morse code?"

As Tish opened her mouth to answer, Kathryn said the words along with her.

"I read it in a book once," they said in unison, and the rest of the crew laughed.

Chapter 23

The light on the panel at Ground Control blinked on and off.

"Shuttle to control, come in," the light signaled, over and over and over, flashing the Morse code message Tish was sending. The light, however, was one of hundreds on the control panel, and no one at Mission Control even noticed that it was blinking.

Back on the ship, Tish sat at a panel, tapping the message over and over, in the hope that someone was going to spot the light. The ship now sat right alongside Daedalus. The computer readout flashed the message: OXYGEN REMAINING: TWENTY MINUTES.

"Okay," Andie said as she floated past the rest of the crew to the air lock door. "I'll be gone twenty minutes. Don't talk any more than you have to, and don't move around unless it's absolutely necessary. Remember that talking and movement use up almost as much oxygen as breathing does."

She floated to the air lock door and pulled it open. "Kathryn," she said, "you're in charge until I get back."

She gave each crew member one last look and floated into the air lock, pulling the entry hatch closed behind her. Kevin locked it from the inside. Then they all watched through the window as Andie prepared to leave the ship.

Her space suit (or Extravehicular Mobility Unit) was mounted on a pipe frame on the air lock wall. She slid the trousers of the EMU over the one-piece Spandex cooling and ventilation garment she was already wearing. The trousers slowed down her movements, so it took longer to get into the EMU upper torso section, connect the water coolant tube to her backpack, and join the top and bottom halves of the suit together. There were no zippers in the suit. The top and bottom halves joined with a connecting ring.

Because of the difference in pressure between the cabin and her space suit, Andie had been breathing pure oxygen from the portable oxygen system before entering the air lock. This had "washed" the nitrogen gas bubbles out of her blood and would keep her from getting the bends.

Now she slipped her head into the communications carrier (also known as the Snoopy hat), adjusted the oxygen flow inside the suit, and pulled on the thick gloves. Finally, she covered her head with the helmet and locked all the connecting rings. She was ready to float out into the cargo bay and then into space.

Kevin was now in the commander's seat, Kathryn in the pilot's position. Tish concentrated on the message she was tapping. Rudy and Max looked out the window in the aft crew station at the spot where Andie would emerge in the cargo bay.

Rudy, too nervous to keep quiet, began running off at the mouth. "You know, I once knew this guy who could hold his breath underwater for hours. Nobody could ever figure out how he did it. Well, maybe it wasn't hours. But it sure was a long time. I was on the swim team with him, that was in freshman year. He used to hold his breath by thinking about eating — "

"Rudy," Kevin said gently over the headset. "You're using up oxygen."

"Yeah," Max said, not so gently. "*Our* oxygen."

Rudy's eyes widened in fear. He swallowed hard and silently turned to look out the window again.

Andie moved out into the cargo bay. She had backed into the jetpack (or Manned Maneuvering Unit) and connected it to her back. Now she spoke into her microphone. "Rudy, do you copy?"

"Yeah, Andie, I copy," Rudy said into his own mike.

"Prepare to open cargo bay doors," she said. "And . . . *go!*"

Tish looked up from her tapping to give him a smile of encouragement. He swallowed again and threw a switch on the panel in front of him. Then he and Max plastered themselves against the windows to watch.

The outside doors of the cargo bay slid open. Andie gasped at the enormous blackness confronting her. Then she hit the MMU jet control and slowly rose out into it.

Seconds later, she floated away from the ship toward the space station. As she spun, she could see Earth below her, the Indian Ocean stretching out for her delight. An incredible feeling of joy swept over her.

"Oh, Zach!" she whispered, trying hard to keep the tears from forming in her eyes.

"Could you repeat that, Andie?" she heard Rudy's voice ask in her headset. "I did not copy."

"Nothing, Rudy," she said loudly into her mike. Then she aimed herself directly at the honeycomb gridlike structure of Daedalus.

Her laughter came into every headset on the ship. It was a giddy sound, reminding them of birthday parties, or roller coaster rides, or childhood experiences they couldn't clearly remember. They exchanged nervous glances, but no one said a word.

Outside, Andie had reached the space station and was now climbing upward, hand over hand, from girder to girder. As she moved, she checked each section of the grid for the oxygen tanks.

When their bright orange color caught her eye, she yelled into her mike, "There they are!"

In her own headset, she could hear the cheers that filled the ship. She moved into the grid chamber that held the two tanks that would get them back home. She was stopped cold at the entrance, too big in her cumbersome space gear for the opening.

"I can't reach them!" she said. "I'll have to remove the MMU."

Slowly, laboriously, she unstrapped the jet-pack from her back and fastened it onto one of the beams of the space station. Then she made the mistake of looking down past the shuttle into the nothingness below. She got dizzy, lost her grip on the beam, and began floating away from it. She recovered in a second, and grabbed the beam.

Andie moved back to the opening and tried again to get at the tanks. She was still too big for the space.

"It's no good," she said. "I can't reach them! I'd have to be half my size!"

The cheers in the ship had now been replaced by near-hysteria. "She has to get them!" Tish screeched. "Tell her she has to!"

"She can't, Tish!" Kevin yelled.

"Make her!" Tish screamed.

"She's just not small enough!" Kathryn said.

They all turned when a tiny voice, mustering as much sarcasm as it could under the circumstances, said, "No kidding."

It was Max, and he was heading toward the air lock. "Where's that other suit?" he asked.

Chapter 24

While the others watched, Max pulled the suit out of the air lock and laid it out on the mid-deck of the ship. Knowing that all eyes were upon him, he left the suit on the deck and floated over to a window. He'd had a feeling this might happen, and he'd begun the special depressurization preparation much earlier.

He looked at the space station, then at Earth. Then he let his eyes roam over the vast emptiness that contained them both. He stared at that emptiness for a long time. Finally, he turned to face the others.

"I can't do it," he said definitively.

"Max, " Kevin said, "you're the only one small enough. Think of it as an adventure! No! It's really a mission! That's it, Max. This is your mission — against the Empire!"

For a second, Max's eyes lit up. Then he smirked at Kevin and said, "You told me that there was no Empire, and no Force!"

"I was wrong, Max," Kevin blurted out. Then, getting control, he straightened his stance and said, "I apologize, Commander Skywalker. I was wrong. Luke, the Princess needs you. Please, you must help!"

Kevin, Tish, Rudy, and Kathryn stared at Max. Before their eyes, he seemed to grow taller. Standing almost at attention, he took a deep breath, nodded, and spoke to all of them.

"I am ready," he said simply.

"Great!" Kathryn said. "And remember, you won't have to use a jetpack. We'll use the Remote Manipulator System and move you from in here."

"Oh, no, not again!" Max wailed.

"All you have to do is sit on the RMS arm and we'll get you from here to Andie," said Rudy.

Minutes later, Max was suited up just as Andie had been earlier. The suit was much too big for him, but the rope that Tish had found came in handy for that problem. They had cut the rope into sections, using each as a belt to pull Max's suit tighter around him in several places. The result was that he looked like a little kid moving about inside a series of white tires.

He floated into the air lock, and Kevin closed the hatch behind him. After exiting the air lock on the other side, but before climbing onto the RMS arm, Max looked out — and up. He saw Daedalus. He saw Earth. And beyond it, he saw nothing but space. His stomach flipped and he turned back to the air lock door.

"I've changed my mind!" they heard him yell, as he pounded on the door. "Let me in!"

"Max!" Kathryn said into her mike, "you have to help Andie!"

Kevin cleared his throat. "Luke," he said solemnly, "remember the Force. Stretch out your feelings, Luke. The Force is always with you."

Max hesitated, then turned away from the air lock door. He silently climbed onto the arm and strapped himself in. Inside the ship, Rudy went over and sat at the RMS controls.

"Ready," Max said.

Rudy moved a lever, and the arm began making its way toward Daedalus. Max made the same mistake Andie had made a few minutes earlier. He looked down — and saw nothing.

"Help me!" they heard his voice cry. "Help me, Obi Wan Kenobi!"

After a few jerky movements, Rudy mastered the controls. Max now moved smoothly toward the space station, where Andie waited for him. She had her jetpack on again.

"I'm Luke Skywalker," Max said coolly, as he reached her. "I'm here to help you."

"You can be anyone you like," Andie said.

"Excuse me," he said, releasing himself from the arm. "I have a mission."

He floated into the storage grid where the oxygen tanks were waiting for him.

Chapter 25

"I'm hurrying, Andie," Max said. "Honest."

"I know you are, Max," Andie said, watching as he undid the fasteners around the tanks. Watching was all she could do, since Max was the only one who could get at the tanks. She kept the crew informed of his progress as he worked.

"That's one tank," she said to her mike. "I'm securing it to the RMS arm, and Max is working on the second tank. We should be finished in no time."

It occurred to Andie that she didn't hear any cheering, or even encouragement. But she had too much work to do without worrying about what was going on back at the ship.

What was going on was that a buzzer had sounded at the same time Andie had given her most recent progress report. The buzzer brought everyone's attention to the computer screen, which displayed a flashing red light.

"Well, that's it," Kevin said, away from his mike. "The air in the cabin is all we have left."

Outside, Max tugged on the second tank to pull it out of the storage grid. It seemed to be stuck on something. As he did so, he let go of the girder he had been holding onto for support.

Suddenly, the tank came loose and Max shot away from the space station, tumbling head over heels, the canister cartwheeling behind him . . . into space.

The crew watched, horrified, through the flight deck window as Andie turned on her jetpack and sailed after Max. Higher and higher she flew, as Max arced further away, almost out of reach. At first it looked as if she would be too late. Then, at the last minute, she reached to the limit and just managed to grab him by the foot. She pulled him in and held him in her arms. The second tank of oxygen floated behind him, secured to his waist by a tether. Andie hit the jetpack again, and she and Max moved back to the RMS arm.

Back at Control, Zach and the director kept track of all the instrument readings, which kept them posted on everything that was going on — inside and outside the shuttle.

"Four minutes to reentry," Zach said, mostly

to himself. "Let's hope they get the oxygen connected."

Once they were back inside the cargo bay, Max and Andie were secured to a rail by a tether. An oxygen tank floated between them, as Andie studied the dozens of valves, tubes, and connections in front of her.

"You've got the tank hose, Andie?" Rudy asked over the headset.

"Yes," Andie said. "Now what do I connect it to, Rudy?"

"Uh — " Rudy hesitated. "The, uh, blue valve."

"Which one?" Andie snapped. "There are two. Rudy, this is pure oxygen, remember? You give me the wrong connection and we'll all be blown to bits! You *must* get it right!"

"It's the blue valve next to the green one," Rudy said confidently.

"There is no blue next to a green!" Andie yelled.

Rudy began flipping through the pages of his manual. He found what he was looking for in seconds, then spoke into his mike.

"Not green! I meant yellow!"

Kathryn came up behind him and grabbed the book from his lap. She looked carefully at the diagram.

"Sorry, Rudy," she said coldly, "we'll all be dead before you make up your mind." Then, into her mike, she said, "Andie, it's the blue valve next to the red."

"You're looking at the wrong diagram!" Rudy screamed.

"No, I'm not," Kathryn said. "Andie, it's the blue valve next to the red."

"Will someone please make a decision?" Andie pleaded into their headsets.

"It's next to the red!" Kathryn shouted.

"And I'm telling you it's next to the yellow!" Rudy said, grabbing the book from her. "This is *my* job. I've been studying this book since Andie left! I know I'm right! Do it, Andie!"

As Max watched, Andie hesitated, weighing the argument she had just heard. Then she moved the tank valve toward the connection Rudy had described. She took a deep breath, snapped the connection on, and hit the valve on the tank.

A sudden whoosh of air inside the ship was followed by a series of loud whoops from Rudy and Tish. As the fans began to hum, they both floated over to a vent to get some new air.

Kathryn stood riveted to the spot next to Rudy's station. Her face was white, and she stared at the diagram in front of her.

Kevin floated up to her. "Well," he said lightly, "red was close. Yeah, I probably would have guessed red, too."

Kathryn didn't move.

* * *

"All right!" Zach cried. "They have air! Now let's bring them home!"

Amid general cheering, he and the launch director sat back down at the panel. Zach watched as the director threw switches and barked orders into his microphone.

Andie took the second tank from Max. She put it in position next to the first one and grabbed the tank hose.

"Okay, Max," she said, holding the tank in place with her stomach. "I have it. Get back in the air lock, and I'll finish here."

Max began floating toward the air lock.

"And Max?" she called. He turned to face her. "Thanks," she added.

He gestured in a sort of salute, turned, and continued on his way. Andie connected the hose from the tank and turned the valve. Suddenly, the hose ripped from the pressure and oxygen began shooting out of the tank like water out of a supercharged garden hose. The effect turned the tank into a minijetpack. First it hit Andie squarely in the stomach, then it shot her down the length of the cargo bay. She hit the far wall with a crash. Max turned, saw what was happening, and screamed.

Inside the ship, the four crew members looked out to see Andie hit the wall and then begin to float slowly up out of the cargo bay. Her tether line, still fastened securely to the rail, was all that kept her from drifting away into space.

Max headed for her tether line. He was just about to pull her back in when a shadow fell across his face. Looking up, he screamed again.

"What's happening?!" he yelled into his microphone.

The crew, horrified, watched as the cargo bay doors closed, leaving Andie floating outside the ship. Inside the ship, Tish read the monitor and announced her own horrifying discovery.

"It must be NASA!" she cried. "They're controlling the ship. They're bringing us down on automatic pilot!"

"Andie, can you hear us?!" Kathryn said frantically. "Andie, come in!"

Andie fought to stay conscious, trying to think about what she might tell the crew to do. As the air inside her suit became heavy, she listened to snatches of the conversation going on inside the ship.

"There's the manual override switch!" Kathryn said. "We can stop the automatic pilot with that!"

"If we override NASA," Kevin said, "we'll miss the window! We have to reenter now!"

"We won't have enough oxygen for the next window!" Rudy reminded everyone.

"But we can't just leave her out there!" Tish said. "She'll die!"

Kathryn realized that everyone else was staring at her. They were waiting for her to make a decision. She looked from Andie, floating outside, to the override switch, and back to Andie again.

They all heard Andie's voice in their headsets. "Take the window, Kathryn," she said weakly. "It's your only chance."

Back on Earth, Mission Control was happily completing its procedure for getting the shuttle back into Earth's atmosphere.

"Stand by for OMS burn," Zach said. "Ten, nine. . . ."

Kathryn and the others stared at the digits flashing on the computer screen just above the override switch. "Eight, seven, six, five — "

"Four," Zach said, "three, two, one — " And nothing happened. The override switch had been thrown.

Chapter 26

Kathryn's hand had frozen in midair above the override switch. With the countdown at two, Kevin had moved beside her and thrown the switch himself.

Now the ship was entirely under their control. Kevin called out a series of orders to get Andie back inside.

"Rudy, open the cargo bay doors! Tish, unstow the medical kit. Max, do you copy? We're opening the doors. Bring Andie in!"

"Okay," Max said. "Just tell me what to do!"

"Just grab onto her tether line when the doors open," Kevin said. "Then pull! Okay, Rudy. Do it!"

Rudy threw the switch that opened the doors, and Tish and Kevin watched as Max yanked Andie back inside the cargo bay.

"Kathryn!" Kevin said. "Run a check on the manual systems. I'd sure hate for this to get any worse than it is."

Kathryn stood staring at the override switch, which she had been unable to throw. Kevin put his hand on her shoulder.

"Kathryn?" he said. "The manual systems."

She looked at him, a bit startled. Then she nodded and got to work.

Max now had Andie inside the air lock. After waiting an agonizingly long time to readjust to the air pressure, Tish unlocked the inside entry hatch, and Max sailed in, pulling Andie's unconscious form behind him.

"Let's get her to the bunk!" Kevin ordered.

Rudy removed Andie's helmet, revealing a chalk white face that scared everyone. As Kathryn got to work with the medical kit, Kevin called over to Tish.

"Any response yet, Tish?"

"Nothing," she said gloomily, tapping her message in Morse code.

"Why would she override automatic?!" Zach shouted, pacing back and forth in front of the control board. "Why would she purposely miss the window? How much oxygen could they have picked up at Daedalus?!"

The launch director shook his head. "Not enough for the next window for Edwards," he said.

"Why would she miss her last chance?" Zach said, knowing that no one at Control had any answer for him. "What else has gone wrong up there?"

Andie was breathing, but unconscious. Max strapped her into the bunk, as Kevin and Rudy watched anxiously.

"If I had been just a little closer to those doors — " Max said.

"You were great, Max," Rudy said softly. "Just like in the movies." ·

Max snorted. "I don't think I like being a hero," he said, sounding years older than when he had begun his mission. Then, back to his normal voice, he asked, "Is she going to be okay?"

"I think she has a broken arm," Kevin said. "Maybe a couple of ribs, too. Now I wish I'd finished that first-aid course at school."

He looked down at Andie for a few seconds. Then he stood up, and again spoke like the commander of the ship.

"Max, stay with Andie. Yell when she comes around. Rudy, let's see what we can find out."

Kathryn sat in the pilot's seat, staring at the darkened Earth below. Were her parents sound asleep? she wondered. Or had NASA told them what was happening to her?

As Kevin and Rudy made their way to the manuals, they passed Tish, still busily tapping out her message.

"Is she going to be okay, Kevin?" Tish asked.

"I sure hope so," Kevin answered. "I just don't know what else to do right now."

Rudy pulled several manuals from a shelf, and Kevin stood at the commander's seat. He looked over at Kathryn.

"Did we make the window?" he said. "No. Do we have enough air for the next window? No. Is Andie going to make it? Who knows? Throwing that switch was a great call, Kevin."

Kathryn stopped thinking about her parents. She turned until she was facing him.

"You did the right thing," she said.

"Sure," he said, forcing a smile. "Look where it got us."

"Andie is part of the crew," Kathryn said, trying to reassure him. "You took responsibility for her. For all of us. *Somebody* had to."

Kevin looked over and saw that she was fighting back tears. He reached out and took her hand.

"I didn't know *what* to do!" she said.

"Who did?" he asked.

"But you decided!" she said. "You did something! You made a decision. That's what a commander does!"

"Come on, Kathryn," Kevin said softly. "Who cares about all that stuff now?"

"I do!" she said, pulling her hand from his. "Andie trusted me! My mom says when people trust you, you *have* to be there!"

"Look," Kevin said calmly. "You did the best you could, okay? Please don't start crying now. We have enough problems without having to worry about drowning."

He put his hand under her chin and lifted it. Her tears floated between their faces, and they both laughed.

"You know," he said, "I was looking for a way of avoiding taking calculus in the fall. This has got to be the stupidest solution anyone could ever imagine."

Kathryn laughed again.

"I hate to break this up, guys," Rudy said, floating up to them. "But I have a question. Is Edwards the only giant lake bed where we can land this thing?"

"No," Kevin said, looking serious. "We could come down in Russia. That would go over big on the six o'clock news."

Rudy scratched his head. "I thought I read somewhere that they landed the shuttle in White Plains."

"In New York?" Kevin asked.

"White Sands!" Kathryn shouted. "White Sands, New Mexico! It was Columbia, in March of '82. The airstrip at Edwards was too wet, so they came in at White Sands!"

Tish stopped tapping to say, "So, if we could make the window to White Sands. . . ."

"We could land there!" Kathryn said excitedly. "Kevin, that might be the answer!"

"Tish," Kevin said, picking up on Kathryn's excitement, "keep at it! *Make* them hear us! Rudy, check out the coordinates. Let's see if we can navigate this bird ourselves."

Kevin watched everyone spring into action. As he moved toward his seat, he let out a whoop.

"Are we unbeatable?" he yelled. "Are we a team, or *what*!?"

Chapter 27

At Control, they were still trying to figure out why Andie would have put the ship on manual just before it reached its window. They were closely monitoring the ship's progress, but they still had no idea why it had passed its window.

What little conversation was going on was muffled and quiet. Everyone sat waiting for something that would make sense of the present puzzle. No one realized that the answer was about to come crashing into the room.

The doors swung open and banged against the walls. Jinx rolled into the control room at top speed, circled the bank of monitors, then came to a screeching halt in front of Zach.

"Jinx put Max into space," Jinx intoned. "Jinx can get Max back."

Zach stared at the robot for several seconds. Then he asked suspiciously, "Jinx, how did you know about Max?"

"FRF to Thermal Curtain Failure," Jinx answered. "Piece of cake."

Zach stared again, this time astounded at what he had just heard. As its meaning began to dawn on him, he turned to the launch director.

"Zach," the director said, "get rid of that thing!"

"No!" Zach said. "It knows something." He turned to Jinx and said, "How can Jinx help NASA?"

Jinx made a series of beeping sounds. Then he spun his dome in a full circle several times, scanning the room and reading the various instruments and monitors. Zach thought he heard something that sounded like "Yo, Max" coming from his speakers.

Jinx stopped spinning his dome and focused on one bank of lights. He rolled over to them, clamped an arm on the panel, and pointed his scanners toward a single blinking light.

As everyone in the room stared at him, Jinx began to chant, "C-O-M-E-I-N — "

"What a time for a malfunction!" the director wailed.

Jinx continued, "C-O-N-T-R-O-L. Come in, Control! Code! Max's code!"

Zach's astonished eyes went from Jinx to the board, where he saw the flashing light. He broke into a broad grin and turned to the director.

"Morse code!" he cried.

Jinx continued, "Request . . . alternate . . . landing. . . . White — "

"White Sands!" Zach said. "Columbia in '82! Get the manuals! Check it out!"

In no time, a technician read from a screen, "White Sands reentry window is nine minutes away."

"Get me White Sands," the launch director said. "Tell them to be ready for a landing in a little over an hour. Andie will have to slow down the ship. Let's transmit."

Tish sat tapping out her message over and over. She stared at her hands, mumbling to herself as she tapped.

"They'll never get this message. I feel like I've been tapping all my life. They'll never read it!"

She didn't see the light that began blinking over her head. She didn't notice when a second light joined it, blinking at the same tempo. Even when five, six, seven lights were blinking in unison, Tish continued to watch her hands.

But when the whole board in front of her was blinking at once, Tish took notice.

"What's going on now?" she whined.

Then she spotted the pattern. The whole board was blinking a Morse code message to her.

"Whip me, beat me, take away my charge plates!" Tish screamed. "It's NASA!"

Everyone rushed to stand behind her as she

read out the message that was blinking in one letter at a time. When they realized that the ship had to be slowed down, Kevin and Kathryn raced back to their seats to follow instructions.

Jinx sat in a chair, watching the humans do what they could to bring Max back home. His scanners whirled, taking in everything that was happening in the room — and, by means of the monitors, in the shuttle.

"Tell Andie to slow down to forty-eight hundred," Zach told the director.

The launch director was writing the latest message coming in from the ship. He looked up and said, "It isn't Andie, Zach. We just got this message. Andie's hurt. Kathryn is flying the shuttle."

Zach stared at him. His lips began to form a question. But no sound came from him. He looked up into the sky.

Chapter 28

The flight deck of the shuttle was now under the tight control of a team. Kevin read the gauges in front of his seat. Tish tapped out messages to NASA and read the incoming messages to Rudy. Rudy relayed the messages to Kathryn, who sat at the computer reading the screen to Kevin.

"Window coordinates 113 by 17," Rudy said.

"Roger," Kathryn replied. "We had figured 250 by 19."

"Well," Kevin said, making a face, "we weren't that far off."

"Time parameter 0210," Rudy said. "We have to be at reentry at 0210." He looked at his watch. "That's six minutes!"

"Max!" Tish called. "Zach wants to know how Andie's doing!"

On the mid-deck, Max held a container of juice, as Andie sipped through a straw. When she moved her body, her face showed the pain she was in.

"Max," she said, "get me a headset."

"She wants a headset!" Max called jubilantly. "I think she's fine!"

"Don't worry, Andie," Kevin called down to her. "We can handle it. You taught us real well."

As he tossed a headset to Max, Tish said, "She taught *us* real well?"

"Not me," Kevin said quietly. "But we'll fake it." He turned to Kathryn and said, "Right, pilot?"

Kathryn sat in her chair, not moving, her eyes closed shut, her fists clenched. "I can't do it, Kevin," she said. "I'm too scared."

"Sure you can do it," Kevin said, climbing into his own chair. "Look, what's the worst thing that could happen? We could all die. But we'll all die if you don't do it. So you have nothing to lose."

"I can't!" she cried.

Kevin took a deep breath and strapped himself in. "No problem," he said, looking over the gauges. "I'll do it. Hey, Tish, did you ever read a book on how to fly this thing?"

Kathryn looked back at Tish, then shot a glance at Kevin. "All right," she said, "I'll do it."

"So competitive," Kevin said, grinning. Then, much louder, he announced, "Okay, team. Helmets on. Let's go for it. Coordinates locked in?"

"Roger," Kathryn said. "Locked in."

"Stand by for OMS burn," Kevin said, as he leaned forward to throw several switches. "Hey, Max!" he added. "We're going home!"

"Great!" Max's voice replied. "I'm starving!"

"OMS burn on my mark," Kevin said. "Three, two, one, *mark*." Kathryn hit the button, and the rockets fired.

The next message from NASA told them they were two minutes from their reentry window.

"Reentry in range," Kevin told the crew. "Prepare for 180 yaw."

"Standing by," Kathryn said.

"And go!" Kevin ordered.

Kathryn twisted the control stick, and the ship began to move into its new path.

"You are looking goood!" Kevin said, as the rest of the crew clapped and whistled.

"Steady," Kathryn said, smiling. "We're passing through 135 degrees. On the way to 180."

She twisted the control stick, and the ship continued to rotate.

"I don't know if we came around enough!" she said, twisting the stick in the opposite direction. "Oh, no, wait a minute!"

"We don't have a minute!" Kevin said. "What's wrong?"

"Look!" Kathryn cried, pointing out the window in front of them.

With Earth in front of them, Kevin could now

see that the shuttle was in a spin, completely out of control.

"Kathryn!" Tish screamed. "Make it stop!"

"You're in a flat spin!" Andie said over the headset. "Kathryn, you must recover!"

"We're coming up on reentry!" Kevin added. "We have to stabilize!"

"I can't!" Kathryn shouted.

"The trainer, Kathryn!" Kevin shouted. "Remember the trainer! You can do it! You did it before!"

Kathryn closed her eyes and pictured the day she had mastered this technique in the trainer. That time, too, she thought she would never get it. But she had brought it under control, through concentration and sheer willpower.

Now she moved the stick, trying desperately to find the center. Slowly, the spin seemed less severe. Earth began to look steadier, and then the spin ended. The ship was again under her control. As they began to stabilize, she reached out and hit the switches, acting without thinking, almost on automatic pilot herself.

"Kathryn," Andie's voice said, "get the nose up. We have to go in at the correct angle."

"Andie, please help me," Kathryn pleaded. "I can't do this!"

"You have to," Andie said firmly. She laid her head back on her pillow, the strain becoming too much for her. Then with her eyes closed, she continued.

"Kathryn, remember that night at camp? When we talked about when it would be your turn? This is it, Kathryn. Go for it."

Kathryn listened to Andie's words. Then she looked over at Kevin. She sat up straight and pushed on the stick.

"Reentry angle should be 30 degrees, at least," Kevin said. "We're at 26 . . . 27 . . . all right, keep going, Kathryn. Now 28 . . . come on, we're almost there, 30!"

"It won't hold!" Kathryn shrieked.

But she was wrong. It did hold, she did maintain control, and the shuttle did break through into the atmosphere. They looked out the window and saw the ocean, then land, then a familiar coastline.

"Oh, man!" Kevin sang. "I *love* L.A.!"

Soon they could see the strip that waited for the latest shuttle landing. Kevin and Kathryn sat smiling in their seats, while Tish and Rudy sat behind them laughing.

"Mode select for auto-land," Kathryn said. "Commander, would you be kind enough to set flap angle for landing?"

"My pleasure, pilot," he replied. "Now where is that control . . . ?"

Exasperated, she sat forward and began reaching for the flap control. Kevin laughingly pushed her hand aside.

"Just kidding," he said, making the adjustment. "Flap angle set. Speed brake at twenty percent."

"Nice work, commander," Kathryn said. They looked at each other and smiled.

"Atlantis!" a frantic voice said on the headsets. "Atlantis, do you copy? Come in, Atlantis! Do you copy?"

"Roger, Control," Kevin said. "Is that you, Zach? This is Atlantis."

They could hear the cheering behind his voice. "Andie!" Zach called. "Andie, are you all right?"

"We're all fine, Zach," Andie said. "And real happy to be home."

"It's so beautiful!" Kathryn whispered, looking at the panorama in front of them.

Tish and Rudy came up behind them to see the view. Rudy hit a switch with his elbow, and the cabin lights went out.

"Oops, sorry," Rudy said, grinning sheepishly. "Got to start dealing with gravity again."

In the darkened cabin, Kevin and Kathryn's faces drew slowly closer, and for an instant, their lips gently touched. Then Rudy switched the lights back on.

"What's happening?" they heard Max ask.

"We're almost home, Max," Kevin said softly. "From here on, you can measure it in seconds."

EPILOGUE

In a quiet neighborhood not far from Phoenix, Arizona, a nine-year-old boy lay stretched out on his back on the roof of his family's garage. As he stared at the sky, he saw a bright light streak across the sky. He propped himself up on his elbows, his jaw hanging open.

"Peter!" his mother called. "Come in and watch it with us. It's on TV. They're almost home!"

Then, as Peter watched, the streak of light disappeared. Seconds later, it was there again.

He stood on the roof. "They winked at me!" he exclaimed. "They winked at me!"

Never taking his eyes from the light, he said, almost in a whisper, "I'm going up."

Then, much louder, as though he wanted the world to hear, he shouted, "I am! I'm going up!"

Summer Blockbusters! from Scholastic *point*™ Paperbacks

Look for them at your bookstore soon!

Coming in June...
HIGH SCHOOL REUNION by Carol Stanley
It's been a year since Jordan, Leigh, Sue, Graham, and Scooter graduated from high school. Now the five old friends return for a reunion that's steaming with deceit, tension, romance, and regrets.
33579-0   **$2.25 US /$2.95 Can.**

Coming in July...
BLIND DATE by R.L. Stine
It wasn't a date. It was a nightmare. Kerry thought it might be fun to go on a blind date—Mandy sounded like a real fox. Too bad Kerry doesn't know that Mandy isn't who she pretends to be...and that she just might kill to go out with him again!
40326-5   **$2.25 US /$2.95 Can.**

Coming in August...
SATURDAY NIGHT by Caroline B. Cooney
Meet **ANNE,** a girl in trouble, abandoned by the boy she loves; **KIP,** organizer of the dance who forgot to line up an escort for herself; **EMILY,** everybody's friend and nobody's date; **MOLLY,** who can buy anything she wants except a good friend. They'll all be at the Autumn Leaves Dance, at eight, on a special **Saturday Night.**
40156-4   **$2.25 US /$2.95 Can.**